# GRANNY BARES IT ALL

## A SECRET AGENT GRANNY MYSTERY BOOK 4

### HARPER LIN

D1563622

This is a work of fiction. Names, characters, organizations, places, events, and incidents are either products of the author's imagination or are used fictitiously.

GRANNY BARES IT ALL

Copyright © 2018 by Harper Lin.

ISBN-13: 978-1987859614

ISBN-10: 1987859618

www.harperlin.com

# ONE

It was supposed to be a routine trip to the super-market to buy cat food for Dandelion, my tortoise-shell kitten, and help my friend Pearl do her own shopping.

But nothing routine ever seems to happen to me.

I'm Barbara Gold. Age: seventy. Height: five foot five. Eyes: blue. Hair: gray. Weight: none of your business. Specialties: Undercover surveillance, small arms, chemical weapons, Middle Eastern and Latin American politics. Current status: Retired widow and grandmother.

Addendum to current status: Realizing that suburban America can hide as many dark secrets as Kabul or Baghdad.

I had retired to Cheerville, thinking it was a dull

town, in order to be close to my son and his family. Instead I had come across murders, an illegal gambling ring, organized crime, and all sorts of lethal hatred and rivalry.

The worst was yet to come.

Well, maybe not the worst, but certainly the weirdest.

So I was driving to the supermarket, singing a little tune to myself as I passed through downtown Cheerville. I was humming in order to drown out Pearl's monologue, which, like all her monologues, was an endless list of everybody's faults. At the moment she was complaining about her nurse, Fatima. Pearl is ninety-six and needs help with many things. Fatima was a patient woman from Nicaragua who cooked, cleaned, and cared for her. Not that Pearl showed any gratitude.

"… so then she put the salt shaker to the right of the pepper shaker. Have you ever heard of such a thing?" Pearl was saying.

"La la la la," I sang. It was a tune of my own making, one that ran as long as Pearl would complain.

"I mean really, the salt shaker goes on the left. It always goes on the left. Maybe it doesn't in Mexico where she's from. Or is it Honduras? One of those countries anyway."

"La la la la."

She couldn't hear my singing. Pearl is as close to deaf as you can get without being a lamppost.

I drove through the historic center of Cheerville, past a large, triangular village green with gnarled old oak trees growing along its edges. Just as gnarled and old as Pearl, but quieter. To one side stood a splendid old Colonial church with a fine white steeple that seemed to touch the sky. Beside the front door, a bronze plaque gleamed in the sunlight. It commemorated a visit by George Washington, who according to local legend, prayed here during the War of Independence. Next to it was an eighteenth-century graveyard where some of his soldiers were buried.

On another side of the green stood a long row of Colonial-style buildings—some old, some imitation—with boutiques and antique shops. The supermarket was about half a mile beyond the village green in a less quaint part of town near the commuter railway station.

Downtown Cheerville's one streetlight turned red just as we came up to it. I stopped, and a woman in her sixties strolled out onto the pedestrian crosswalk in front of me.

Just then, a car that had been idling in front of

the antiques shops roared out of its parking place, shot past me, and slammed right into the woman.

She flipped over the hood of the car, crashed into the windshield, rolled over the roof, and smacked hard on the pavement.

"Oh my God!" I shouted.

"Ouch," Pearl said.

The car kept on going.

"Well, he's sure in a hurry," Pearl commented.

I glanced at the woman. She was obviously dead. Her neck was at an unnatural angle, as were two of her limbs. Looking back at the car that had hit her, I saw it was picking up speed, heading out of the town center. It had already gotten far enough that I couldn't see the license plate.

I hit the gas and went after it.

"You just ran a red light," Pearl said.

"I need to get the license number of that hit-and-run driver."

"Aren't you going to help that lady back there?"

"No one can help her now."

"That's rather cynical. People can change, you know."

"Unless she's going to turn into a zombie, she's not going to do any changing that will see her up and about."

The car was a Lexus and had a better engine than my little old Toyota. The Lexus was already going sixty in a thirty-mph zone and took on a sudden burst of speed, no doubt because the driver noticed I was following. Unfortunately, I couldn't see the driver or even whether there was more than one person in the car because it had tinted windows.

The Lexus passed another car and swerved back into our lane to avoid a van moving the other direction. As soon as the van went by, I passed the car in front and tried to gain on the Lexus. It had pulled farther ahead.

We had left the town center behind us now and were zipping past a few homes and shops. The Lexus took a right off the main road leading to the train station and instead went along a winding, two-lane country road. It went past a housing development and then on to a less built-up area. At least we had left most of the people behind. The way the Lexus was going, it was going to hit someone else if it stayed in town.

No matter how much I tried, my sensible little four-cylinder engine simply could not keep up with the Lexus. I lost sight of it on the curves. On every straightaway, I saw it had pulled a little farther ahead.

"Are you going to follow this person all day?" Pearl asked.

"Yes, if I have to."

"I'm going to be late for my bridge club."

"People still play bridge?"

"There's quite an active group at the Seniors' Center."

On the next straightaway, it had put enough distance between us that I was about to give up.

At least I would have until nature gave a helping hand.

A white-tailed deer bounded out of the woods right in front of the Lexus.

"Bambi! No!" Pearl cried out.

She had a soft spot for deer and proudly said that seeing *Bambi* in the theater when it first came out had been a defining moment of her life, although she was so old she must have graduated from college by that time.

The Lexus swerved to avoid the animal, not from any charitable intentions on the part of the driver but because a good-sized deer can total a car. It's a little-known fact that deer cause more fatalities than any other animal in the United States— more than scorpions, more than rattlesnakes, more than dogs, and way more than sharks. Sharks hardly kill anyone. Not that I'd go swimming with them or anything, but they are a much-maligned creature.

The Lexus swerved into the left-hand lane, nearly wrapped itself around a tree, and cut back into our lane, leaving a set of curving black tire marks as it did so.

The driver adjusted too much, however, and the wheels on the right side ploughed up dirt and gravel on the side of the road. The deer ran into the woods, flicking by us as a brown-and-white blur.

After a few seconds, the driver had regained full control of the Lexus and got back on the pavement. The whole thing had slowed him or her down, though, and I got close enough to check the license plate. It was from our state, and I started reciting the plate number to myself to make sure I remembered it.

Suddenly I got a closer look at the license plate than I wanted to. The driver unexpectedly slammed on the brakes, and I nearly rear-ended the Lexus. The Lexus slowed further, trying to get beside me.

The intent was obvious—the driver wanted to run me off the road, preferably into a tree.

Luckily, I'd been trained in evasive driving when I was in the CIA. A hard foot on the brakes, a swerve to the left, a touch on the gas, and our roles were reversed. If I had been alone, I would have knocked the Lexus off the road myself, but I didn't want to risk a collision with a ninety-six-year-old woman in the passenger's seat.

The driver of the Lexus realized they'd been outmaneuvered and decided discretion was the better part of valor. They hit the gas again, and I began losing ground. I let it go. I had the plate number, and that was good enough for now. I slowed down and drove for another mile to make sure the Lexus wasn't going to turn around and come after us, and then I headed back for the town center.

"Well, that was exciting," Pearl said. "Can we go to the supermarket now?"

"One minute," I muttered, pulling out my phone and writing down the license plate number in the Notes app.

"You shouldn't text while driving," Pearl advised. "You might end up hitting someone like that maniac you were chasing."

I didn't answer, already lost in my own thoughts. That had not been an accident by some idiot who was texting while driving, and that had not been your usual hit and run, where an accident turns into a crime because the driver panics and drives off.

No, that had been cold-blooded, deliberate murder.

## TWO

When we got back to the town center, a small circle of people had gathered around the body in the street. I parked in front of the antiques shop—right where the Lexus had been idling a few minutes before—and left Pearl as I went to check out the scene.

A middle-aged man was kneeling by the body, feeling for a pulse.

Just as I got there, he stood up and shook his head.

"She's dead," he said.

"Are you a doctor?" I asked. He had the precise touch and immaculate hands common to medical personnel.

"No, a dentist, but I'm trained in CPR and first aid. Those won't do any good for her, I'm afraid."

A police siren wailed in the distance. Someone had called 9-1-1.

The police and paramedics were on the scene in less than ten minutes after the hit and run. It didn't take long for the ambulance crew to confirm what the dentist had said. She had been killed in the initial collision.

Now I don't want to give the wrong impression of Cheerville's emergency services. Yes, they had made it to the scene in less than ten minutes, but the police station stood just off the village green, and the hospital wasn't much farther away. Any first responders worthy of their name would have been there in half that time.

But Cheerville's first responders aren't used to emergencies like this. It's supposed to be a sleepy suburban oasis away from the crimes of the big city, a place where commuters can come home and feel safe with their families, a place where retirees can walk the streets at night without fear.

Yeah, right.

While one policeman taped off the lane of the road where the body lay, set up traffic cones, and started directing traffic, his partner took statements from a couple of witnesses who saw the hit and run and from the dentist, who hadn't seen it but had come on the scene a couple of minutes later. Then it was my turn. I gave them a description of the Lexus and the license plate number and said I wanted to press charges for the driver trying to run me off the road while I was in pursuit.

The policeman, a young man in his early thirties who was already developing a donut belly, shook his head.

"Ma'am, you shouldn't have taken the law into your own hands. You might have gotten hurt. You should leave this sort of thing to trained professionals."

I wondered how he would have done in a firefight with the enforcers of a Colombian drug cartel. Not well, I imagined.

Another police car pulled up, and the least efficient officer of Cheerville's inefficient police force got out—Arnold Grimal, the chief of police.

While I never liked seeing this arrogant paper pusher, the look on his face when he spotted me was worth nearly getting run off the road by a murderer.

"What are you doing here?" he demanded.

The epitome of tact, that's Grimal.

"I witnessed the hit and run and pursued the vehicle. I got a license plate number and a description of the car that I gave your officer here."

I made a point of leaning over the officer's

shoulder and reading what he had written on his notepad.

"Yep, he wrote it down right."

The cop frowned at me. Grimal decided to ignore my comment. He would like to ignore my existence entirely. No such luck.

"What possessed you to chase a hit-and-run driver?" he asked.

"A sense of justice. Also, it wasn't a hit and run, it was premeditated murder."

"Murder?" the dentist exclaimed. I hadn't noticed him still standing there.

"Come with me," Grimal growled.

We walked a little apart. He spun on me.

"Why do you have to plague me with things like this? Why can't you just have an uneventful retirement?"

"I often ask myself the same question."

"Death seems to cling to you."

I thought about Afghanistan. Lebanon. El Salvador.

"You have no idea."

He paused, sighed, put his hands on his hips.

"So why was it murder?" he asked in an impatient tone.

Nice choice of words. He didn't ask, "Why do you think it was murder?" He had already decided I was right. I guess after my being right and his being wrong more times than I could count, he had finally given in.

"I was at the intersection, waiting for a red light, when she crossed right in front of me. The Lexus was idling right over there—" I pointed to the parking spot where my car was now. I could just see Pearl's white perm peeking over the dashboard like a giant marshmallow. "It pulled out, picked up speed, rammed right into her, and took off."

Then I gave a detailed description of the chase. Grimal listened in silence.

When I finished, he pulled out his phone and told me to wait. Then he placed a call to the station.

"Linda, could you give me the license number of that Lexus that got stolen this morning?"

The Lexus was stolen? This was getting interesting.

Grimal's groan told me what Linda's answer was. What could have been an open-and-shut case had just gotten a lot more complicated.

"So someone stole a Lexus this morning to use in the murder?" I asked when he hung up.

He nodded. "A couple on the edge of town noticed their car missing this morning. They had it parked in the driveway. Last looked at it about ten o'clock last night and noticed it was gone at seven this morning."

"You'll want to check on their story, of course, but they're not behind this."

Grimal shook his head. "I'm afraid not."

I turned to the woman lying in the street. The paramedics had covered her with a sheet. The scene still needed to be photographed.

"And who is she?" I asked.

The officer who took my statement walked up with her purse. He turned to me.

"That's all, ma'am. Thank you for your help."

I was being dismissed. I don't like being dismissed. I gave Grimal a significant look and stood my ground.

The chief of police took the purse.

"Thank you, Officer Wilkins. I'll take it from here. You go deal with crowd control."

Wilkins gave his boss and me a curious look and walked away without saying anything.

"You're learning," I told Grimal with a grin.

"Learning that you're like a bad penny that I'll never get rid of? Yeah, I've sure learned that."

"So let's see what we have."

He opened the purse and found the usual things like makeup and Kleenex and car keys. The wallet inside contained her identification.

Clarissa Monell. Age: sixty-two. The license showed a Cheerville address. I made a mental note of it. Besides the license there were several other cards—two credit cards, social security, health insurance (oh, the irony!), a membership card to a local gym, and a card for something called Sunnydale Nature Resort. This was printed on cardstock and had a member identification number, her name, but no address for the resort. I found that odd. I also found the logo odd—it showed a silhouette of a man and woman raising their arms to a sunny sky. The man and woman looked nude. Of course, since they were drawn in silhouette, it was impossible to say for sure, but that certainly seemed to be the impression the artist was trying to convey.

Grimal didn't seem to take much note of it and put all the cards back in the wallet.

"We'll take a look into it," he said. He sounded as dismissive as his officer but with a hopeful strain to his voice.

Hopeful that I would allow myself to be dismissed.

"Yes, we will take a look into it," I replied.

Grimal got a pained look on his face, like his pants were too tight in all the wrong places.

"This is a police matter," he said, his voice quavering.

"He tried to run me off the road. Or she. Mustn't be sexist, even though the majority of murderers are men. When we catch him or her or it, I'd like to press charges for attempted murder."

Grimal nodded. "Fair enough. I'll file the paperwork when we catch him. Or her."

He just didn't get it, did he? All these little evasions would get him nowhere.

I decided to let him think he had shaken me off. He could do his investigation and I'd do mine, and I'd call him when I needed him. He'd already been given a good talking to by the head of the Central Intelligence Agency, so he wouldn't dare say no to me when the time came. In the meantime, I'd let him maintain a healthy blood pressure.

It was time for me to get back to Pearl anyway. I wished him luck on his investigation and headed back to the car.

When I got there, I found Pearl asleep, her chin resting on her bodice, snoring contentedly.

# THREE

I may be a sweet little old lady (at least superficially), but I try to keep up with the times as much as possible. So the first place I started my investigation was where everyone looks things up these days—the Internet. Clarissa Monell was an unusual enough name that she proved easy to track down. She had a Facebook account, which unfortunately was set on private, so I couldn't see anything other than her profile photo. It showed her on a hill somewhere. There were grass and wildflowers all around, and she wore hiking boots, shorts, a T-shirt, and a small daypack. She stood with her face to the sun and her arms uplifted. The pose reminded me of the logo on that card in her wallet.

Other than that, I found her on Yelp, which gave the address I already knew from her driver's license, and some older pages that showed she had been a Parks and Recreation official upstate before she retired two years ago at age sixty. That might prove helpful. As she had been a state employee, there would be a lot more records on her. Perhaps they might hold a clue as to why someone would want to run over a Parks and Recreation employee who had opted for early retirement.

Next I looked up Sunnydale Nature Resort and got a shock.

It was a nudist colony. The website showed men and women swimming in a lake, playing volleyball, riding horses, and lounging by a pool, all without a stitch of clothing on.

Cheerville had a nudist colony? I had begun to accept the fact that an inordinate number of people got murdered here and that it had been the location for a secret casino run by organized crime, but a nudist colony? My respectable, boring, mundane neighbors were baring it all and doing … what, exactly? I had a hard time believing people would join a special club just for the opportunity to get a sunburn in all the wrong places.

I had to admit I didn't know much about nudism, or naturism, or nakedism, or whatever you call it. It was also becoming apparent that I didn't know much about sleepy middle-class commuter towns.

For nearly thirty years, my husband and I had traveled the globe, hunting down enemies of the state and protecting our country. I've been to every continent except Antarctica, have a smattering of a dozen languages, and met everyone from narcotraffickers to double agents to Third World dictators. I've camped in the Himalayas, trekked through the Amazon, ridden a boat up the Nile, and snuck into Siberia. I thought I was worldly.

Now I was beginning to realize there are different ways to be worldly. Perhaps it doesn't surprise most people to hear that there's a nudist colony near their town. It made me nearly fall off my chair.

So Clarissa Monell had a weird hobby, if you can call it such. But that didn't mean she got killed for it. This was just one aspect to her life, and I had to look into all of them.

Next I looked up the gym she had belonged to —Suburban Fitness. It looked like your standard gym. Not one of those twenty-four-hour power-lifting places where pneumatically muscled men eat powdered protein and bench-press elephants at three o'clock in the morning but a regular gym for regular people. It even showed up in their marketing, with photos depicting a carefully chosen group of "gym members" of all ages and both sexes. They all had the same pasted-on grins. Nobody grins while running on a treadmill. I suspected they were models.

Even so, I decided to check it out. I had planned to join a gym anyway.

A seventy-year-old woman joining a gym? Some people might think I was too old, but you're never too old to stay in shape. Seniors actually need to exercise as much as or even more than young people. During my CIA days, I had been in tip-top shape, but since retirement I had been letting myself slip a bit. Old battle injuries had begun to hurt again, and despite having been in tip-top shape for much of my life, my physical condition had deteriorated to an alarming degree. I had tried yoga at the Seniors' Center, and besides getting a boyfriend out of it, I didn't find it terribly interesting. A good jog and some weights are more my style.

So I fed Dandelion, who stopped clawing the sofa to pieces to leap on the food, and headed out.

Suburban Fitness was in a strip mall at the edge of town. It turned out to be one of those gyms where everyone wanted to show off how much they were exercising. The ground floor had floor-to-ceiling windows. Right behind the glass was a long line of treadmills and rowing machines. Sweaty men and women worked out in full view of the parking lot. It seemed a bit silly to me. No one looks good when they exercise. Well, not most people anyway. Most were middle-aged and looked like they desperately needed to be there. The only person in view who was young and fit was a lovely girl in black Spandex using one of the treadmills. She was quite shapely and had obviously forgotten to put on a sports bra judging from her, um, vertical movement. I spotted her from halfway across the parking lot.

The two men on the treadmills to either side of her were getting a good view too. They weren't even trying to hide their staring. Both had identical postures, running in place while their heads were turned toward her, angled ever so slightly in a fruit-less attempt at subtlety, eyes straining in their sockets to look to the side in order to get as full a view as possible. A perfect triptych of male desire and female indifference.

Because surely she realized the effect she was having? Did she really want the attentions of a pair of men old enough to be her father? As long as they looked and didn't touch, I suppose she did.

Entering the gym, I came to a front desk where

two spectacularly muscled young men sat. One was tapping away at a computer. Another was tapping away at a cell phone. Neither looked like he was working.

I stood in front of them, counting up to thirty seconds, waiting to be noticed. I decided not to clear my throat. I was curious how long it would take. Consider it a social experiment.

It took a full minute.

At last the guy on the phone looked away from his screen long enough to grab his coffee and noticed me.

"Oh, hello, ma'am, can I help you?"

"Yes, I wanted to ask about membership."

I half expected him to reply with, "Oh, for your son?" but to his credit he said, "What kind of workout are you looking for, ma'am?"

"Basic maintenance. I'd like to stave off inevitable mortality for at least another decade."

He didn't bat an eye. "Well, let me show you around."

When he stood, I saw he was even more impressively muscled than I'd thought, his chest and shoulders on show thanks to one of those cutoff T-shirts that look too drafty to really be called clothing. As he came around to my side of the counter, I also saw he had huge calves. This guy obviously did a lot of squats. I'm not sure why one would need huge calves in this modern world. Perhaps he thought it would attract women, although he had certainly gone too far. I knew Marines who did forced marches of fifty miles a day who didn't have calves like that.

I followed his calves, which looked like two hairy loaves of bread, as he gave me a tour of the facilities. They had a sizeable weight room with all new equipment, and the ladies' room (Mr. Super Calves didn't go in) had a sauna and steam room. It turned out the first impression I had gotten from the window was not entirely correct. There were a fair number of young people here, pulling and pushing and heaving and sweating. And flirting. Lots and lots of flirting. The flirting, however, was strictly divided by age. The twenty-somethings only flirted with other twenty-somethings, the thirty-somethings only flirted with other thirty-some-things, the middle-aged people only flirted with other middle-aged people while ogling the twenty-somethings, and the seniors focused on their workouts.

"We also have classes," Mr. Super Calves said, and led me to a pair of large back rooms with padded floors. One was not being used, while the other had three lines of people facing a wall entirely covered with a mirror. A female instructor up front bounced around while leading them in a series of kicks and punches as some awful electronic music thudded out a synthetic beat.

"What's this?" I asked.

"Muay Thai cardio kickboxing."

I chuckled. I'd learned some kickboxing as part of my hand-to-hand combat training. This wasn't even recognizable as Muay Thai. It was too flashy and bouncy and in time with the beat. While the kids did look like they were getting a good cardio workout, I hoped they didn't think they were learning how to fight. Most of them had their thumbs tucked inside their other fingers when they made a fist. That's a good way to dislocate your thumb.

"We also have seniors' yoga," he said.

"I've tried that. It's just like Muay Thai cardio kickboxing."

He cocked his head. "Really?"

"Yes, the guys all take the back rows so they can see the women's butts, and they can check out their fronts in the mirror."

"Um … "

"It's all right. We're used to it. I picked up a boyfriend at my last seniors' yoga class. He always took the back row too."

Mr. Super Calves looked like my thirteen-year-old grandson any time I brought up adult topics. Mortified, in other words. People with gray hair were supposed to be asexual.

We went back to the counter, and he showed me a list of the classes they offered. None of them interested me. What I needed was a moderate amount of jogging and some weight training. At my age, it's important to get some cardiovascular exercise and a bit of muscle toning. Mr. Super Calves tried to get me a personal trainer, saying that "our senior clients can really benefit," but I didn't need one. I already knew all this stuff; I simply hadn't been applying it for a few years.

To be honest, I had let myself go a bit after my husband, James, died. He had been my lover, comrade-in-arms, and best friend for most of my adult life, and losing him felt like that life had been wiped out. For a couple of years, I had become more or less a couch potato, but then I pulled myself up by my bootstraps and strode back into life.

All right, that's an overstatement. I gently tugged on my bootstraps and tiptoed back into life. The first and best thing I did was move to Cheerville to be close to my son and his family. James's death had left me profoundly alone, and I needed to be close to people I cared about. I still lived alone, however, so I had filled up that gap with a kitten. Then I filled out my social life by joining a reading group and starting to date again.

Now I needed to work on the physical side. I hadn't done much exercise since James passed, and when I saw that gym card in poor Clarissa Monell's wallet, I realized that was the last aspect of life I needed to step back into.

So I left the gym with the proud status of being the newest member of Suburban Fitness. At my age, it feels good to be the newest of anything. I felt like I was getting somewhere. I needed a gym membership anyway, and I'd be interested to see how the clients and staff reacted when Clarissa Monell's death appeared in tomorrow's papers.

Hopefully I'd find some good leads, because the only other lead I had was a nudist colony, and I certainly wasn't going to join that too. I needed to step back into life, but there were limits.

# FOUR

After witnessing a cold-blooded murder, there's nothing better than to sit down and have a nice dinner with your family.

My son, Frederick, his wife, Alicia, and my thirteen-year-old grandson, Martin, lived in a lovely New England–style home with a white picket fence and a couple of trees in the yard. The house stood at the end of a quiet cul-de-sac in a fashionable part of town. Frederick worked in real estate and had gotten himself quite a deal. He'd gotten a good deal on his wife too. Alicia was one of the world's leading particle physicists and spent much of her time working at the CERN reactor beneath the border of France and Switzerland. I didn't really understand what she did for a living. That was OK, because ninety-nine point nine nine percent of the population didn't understand it either.

Luckily, Alicia was home that evening, so dinner would be edible. Frederick is a terrible cook, a trait he inherited from his parents. Taking his son out for hamburgers and fries is actually the healthier option.

Frederick opened the door. My sweet little boy was now in his early forties, with a beer belly and a heavy step. While he had taken after James and me with the cooking, he had not followed our path to physical fitness. I worried about that sometimes. He gave me a hug.

"Hey, Mom, come on in. Dinner's almost ready."

A ready smile and a genuine happiness to see me—that was why I had moved to Cheerville.

We walked into the living room and straight into a warzone.

My grandson Martin was slouched on the couch, eyes nearly invisible under a mop of blond hair as he played *Urban Slaughter V*, which was "much, much better" than *Urban Slaughter IV* but "not as awesome but better graphics" than *Shopping Mall Slaughter, Zombie Edition*. "Just look at how the blood spatters on this wall."

The plots of all the *Urban Slaughter* series were as simple as they were bloody. You ran around the city gathering guns and ammo and shooting gang members, Islamic terrorists, invading Chinese soldiers, chainsaw-wielding serial killers, and crazed drug addicts. Yes, all of these enemies were at large in the city at the same time. Oddly, regular citizens went shopping, ran businesses, and drove on the roads as if nothing was happening. They only reacted if you shot them, then they screamed and you lost points.

Even though Martin was an ace at video games, he never got a good score in *Urban Slaughter* because he shot too many civilians.

"They're funny when they scream," he explained.

I called out a hello to Alicia, who was bustling around the kitchen with her neck crooked to hold a cell phone while both her hands were busy with preparing the meal. Judging from the incomprehensible technobabble coming from her mouth, it was a work call.

"I'll go help her," Frederick said.

"Just wash the dishes," I advised.

My son rolled his eyes in a very teenaged fashion. "You're one to talk."

Middle-aged son: one, Granny: zero.

I sat on the sofa beside my grandson and tousled his unruly shock of blond hair.

"You ruined my aim," he grunted.

"Watch the windows on your right flank. They make a good sniper position," I told him.

He ignored me. A terrorist popped up in one of the windows, ululated a poor imitation of Arabic (which I speak, thank you very much), and took out Martin with a headshot.

"I told you," I said.

Martin gave me a funny look. He always did that when I let slip bits of knowledge grandmothers aren't supposed to have. I bit my lip. All my life I have been very careful to hide my secret identity. Even my son has no idea what I and his father had done for a living. All he knew was that we had worked for the government in "foreign development" and that meant we traveled a lot.

Somehow I had begun to slip with Martin. I suppose that was because he was still half a child, and the knowledge of my past wasn't as secret as it used to be. And, let's be honest here, I wanted to impress him.

"Dinner time!" Alicia's voice cut off any further slaughter on the streets of America. It amused me to see these games. I had spent my whole life stopping this sort of thing from happening, and now kids pretended it really had. Perhaps I should have been a librarian. Then Martin could shoot terrorists and Latin American drug gangs for real. He could do it. In the course of my work, I'd come across soldiers younger than he was.

He'd need to work on his situational awareness, though. He kept getting taken out by snipers who used the terrain better than he did.

We gathered around the table to share the roast chicken Alicia had prepared, and I slipped into the easy, friendly conversation we shared at these times. This is something I had not gotten enough of when I was Frederick's age, and I felt fortunate that I had a chance to catch up now.

"I joined a gym today," I announced. "Suburban Fitness."

Martin looked up from shoveling food into his mouth. "A gym? You?"

I smiled at him. "Grandmas need to keep fit."

"You going to lift weights?" Martin said.

"Of course. Give me a few weeks and we'll have an arm-wrestling competition."

Martin snickered and went back to his meal.

"I wish I had time to go," Alicia said.

"Any trips coming up?" I asked. There usually were with her.

"Five days in L.A. at the end of the month. Ten

days in Germany the next month. And I have to go to the city next week, but that's only a one-day thing."

I nodded. That was actually a light travel schedule by her standards.

Turning to my son, I asked, "Why don't you join me in the gym?"

Martin laughed. "You could spot Grandma. How much can you bench press, Grandma?"

*Three sets of ten reps of my own weight, when I was your father's age,* I remembered. Out loud I said, "Oh, I don't know. It's best to start small and work your way up."

"I want to see you and Dad arm wrestle," Martin said, bouncing up and down in his seat.

Frederick was still shoveling food into his mouth. He hadn't answered my question. I knew well enough not to ask a second time.

Alicia turned to me. "Can you still take care of Martin the night after tomorrow?"

"Oh right, your anniversary. I'd nearly forgotten." Witnessing a murder tended to reprioritize your thoughts.

"We'll go to Fatberger," Martin said. "You won't even need to cook."

The poor child had suffered through some of my attempts at cooking.

"It'll take a dozen workouts to get rid of one dinner at that place," I objected.

While most fast food chains tried to play down how unhealthy their meals were, Fatberger reveled in it and made it the center of their marketing. No, it's not spelled Fatburger, but Fatberger. A fatberg is a phenomenon they are experiencing over in England. The congealed fat of hamburgers, fries, and kebabs is getting glommed together with baby wipes to make giant "fatbergs" like icebergs that clog up the sewer system. Some are as big as a double-decker bus. Fatberger's logo is a giant fatberg with a smiley face holding a bacon double cheeseburger and a milkshake.

"We'll see about Fatberger," I told Martin and turned to my daughter-in-law. "Yes, I can take care of him. You two have a nice evening. What are your plans?"

Frederick shrugged. "Dinner and a movie."

"At Fatberger?" Martin asked.

"No," Frederick said. "That place gives me gas."

Martin screwed up his face. "Eeew. Good thing Grandma is taking me."

I didn't like the idea of having Martin around when I was on a murder investigation, but I had already promised and couldn't see a way to get out of it. It was only for one night, though.

The following afternoon, I went to Suburban Fitness, arriving around 12:30 p.m. to catch the lunchtime crowd. I wanted it to be busy so I could meet as many people as possible. I also wanted to give enough time for news of Clarissa Monell's death to circulate.

When I got there, the first thing I saw was a newspaper report about her death posted in the front hall. A small crowd of people stood reading it, openmouthed.

I joined them, taking a close look at each face and registering every reaction, and saw nothing suspicious.

Everyone had the expected responses—surprise, shock, disbelief, and sadness—none of it very deep. Their emotions were those that any decent person would have at hearing of a tragedy that didn't closely affect them.

My impressions were confirmed by their conversation.

"So who was this?" a young man asked.

"Clarissa. She always used the rowing machine."

"Oh right, I think I remember her."

"Wasn't she in the yoga class?"

"No, you're thinking of Clarice."

"Oh."

"I knew her a bit," a woman in her forties said. She had the harried look of an overworked professional. She reminded me of my daughter-in-law. "We chatted a few times in the sauna. Nice person."

"What a pity. I wonder if the driver was drunk."

"Probably. Says here he went right through a red light."

I read the article, which had been cut out of the front page of the *Cheerville Gazette*. Not much happens in Cheerville, at least on the surface, so her death had earned a banner headline.

Despite its prominent placement, the article wasn't terribly long. It simply stated the bare facts, leaving out my chase and the important detail that the car had been stolen. Grimal had done that part of his job well, at least. He'd gotten the newspaper to play ball. Anyone who hadn't been there would think it was a simple hit and run.

"What a tragedy. Did you know her well?" I said, turning to the woman who had spoken to Clarissa in the sauna.

She shook her head sadly. "No. We talked a few times about regular things, workouts and the news. Did anyone know her better?"

Everyone shook her head.

"She sort of kept to herself," one man ventured.

Interesting. That was a rather odd description of a nudist. I figured that nudists would be more outgoing. If you were uninhibited enough to take your clothes off in public, then I would think you'd be pretty open and social. But I realized that was just a guess. What did I know about nudists?

The crowd broke up, people heading to the machines or out of the gym and back to their daily round. Poor Clarissa was just another minor bit of bad news, something to shake your head over and forget. What a shame that we are all like that on some level. I had seen enough death to know this. When the *Cheerville Gazette* posted my obituary sometime in the hopefully far future, most of those reading it would have no idea who I was. Of those who would—the hairdresser and the nice young man who helped carry my groceries at the super-market and the owner of the shooting range outside of town—they would do little more than heave a sad sigh and get on with their lives.

But I couldn't do that with Clarissa Monell. She had been killed right in front of me, and then her killer had tried to kill me and Pearl. I couldn't just sigh and get on with my life. This stranger's life had become intertwined with mine.

It was the same attitude that had made me join

the CIA. I had studied international relations in university and was an avid news junkie. Even before I got into the CIA, I knew how dangerous the world was and saw clearly the many threats to our country and the rest of the free world. I couldn't stand by and let others do the work while I and everyone I cared about were in danger. I couldn't stand by and allow injustice.

So here I was in the victim's gym, trying to find out more about her.

That turned out to be very little. I lingered in the locker room, eavesdropping on the small talk as I took my time getting changed. Only a bit of it was about Clarissa, and all of that was in the most general terms. Chatting with a few people as I made my rounds of the treadmill and some weights, I found that what the young fellow in the front hall had said had been true. Clarissa Monell kept herself to herself. People who remembered her at all remembered her as a friendly but quiet woman. After my workout, lounging in the sauna and enjoying the sensation of the heat soaking into sore muscles that hadn't been exercised in far too long, I learned the only juicy detail anyone had to share— that Clarissa would sit in the sauna totally naked. Everyone else, myself included, kept a towel wrapped around themselves.

"Perhaps she was a nudist," I said jokingly to the three women sitting with me in the sauna.

"Oh, I wouldn't say that!" one exclaimed.

"It wasn't like she did her workout naked," tittered another.

"You shouldn't speak ill of someone who has just passed," another said, frowning at me.

The gym appeared to be a dead end. Since I planned on going every day, I would keep my eyes and ears open, but I didn't hold out much hope. That left only two possible ways forward, neither of them good—Police Chief Grimal and the nudist colony.

# FIVE

After my workout, I went to visit Grimal. I found him sitting like the desk jockey he was behind a computer, surrounded by file folders, heaps of notes in messy handwriting, and several empty Chinese takeaway boxes.

"Have a good lunch?" I asked, closing his office door behind me without being invited.

He grunted at me. It was his way of saying he didn't like my attitude. That was quite all right; I didn't like his.

"So what have you found out about my attempted murderer?"

"We're pursuing several leads."

"Such as?"

Grimal sighed, looked longingly at the empty

takeaway boxes, no doubt wishing they were full, and said, "What I tell you is privileged information. At the moment, we've told the press that it was a simple hit and run. We don't want to spook the murderer."

"The murderer knows I followed the Lexus and must have figured I got the license plate."

"That won't do any good," Grimal said with a dismissive wave of his hand. "We found the vehicle and dusted it for prints. The steering wheel and driver's-side door had been wiped. Someone didn't want to leave any fingerprints. We dusted the whole vehicle and sent the results to the lab to compare with the owners' prints, but it doesn't look like there's much hope in that direction."

"Where did you find the car?"

"In a parking lot in a strip mall out on the Interstate. No doubt the murderer had their own car parked there and used it to get away. It's too far from anything to walk."

"CCTV?"

"None pointing to that part of the parking lot or the entrance to the parking lot."

"Our murderer is careful."

Grimal nodded. "Yeah, a real pro."

"Professional? Probably not. Running someone over in the center of town is too showy for a professional. Also, too many things can go wrong. The police station is just a hop, skip, and a jump away, and there were bound to be witnesses."

Grimal shrugged. "Perhaps the murderer wanted to be showy. Prove to someone besides Clarissa Monell that you can be vulnerable anywhere and at any time."

I nodded. "You might have a point there."

He sat back, a smug smile on his lips that I had conceded to him. But he did have a point. I was secure enough to allow him his little victories. They were rare enough.

"Other things suggest a pro," he went on in an annoyingly lecturing tone. "He or she picked a car with tinted windows, knew just when Monell would be passing through town, and showed a sense of calm and cold-bloodedness."

"That makes them careful and nasty, not necessarily a pro. When he or she tried to run me off the road, they did it like an amateur. The Lexus was a much more powerful and heavier car than mine. It would have been easy to knock me into a tree if the driver had any training to compete with mine."

Grimal shifted in his seat. He didn't like to be reminded that I was far better trained than he was.

"Did you check out the gym and that … other membership card she had?" I asked.

Grimal actually blushed at that, which told me he had given Sunnydale Nature Resort a visit. He didn't meet my eye when he replied.

"I, um, looked into both organizations. I'm handling this personally, you know, because I'm the most experienced officer." Did I sense a need for justification in his tone? "According to the folks in the gym, she kept to herself mostly. Few people knew her there. And at the … other place, they say she was well liked and had been a member for years."

"Did you tell these people you were investigating a murder?"

"No, of course not. We want to lure the murderer into a false sense of confidence. I stressed that it was routine to ask around after a hit and run like this but that we suspected it was merely a tragic accident with the driver panicking and leaving the scene."

"What other leads do you have?"

"I checked on the couple who had their car stolen. They don't own another vehicle, so I don't see how they could have done the switching routine in the parking lot. Plus neither of them is a member of the gym or the resort."

I bit my lip. "No, I didn't think they would be

mixed up in this. Only a fool would do this with their own car, and we are not dealing with a fool."

Grimal's eyes went wide as he noticed some sweet and sour chicken congealed in the bottom of one of the cartons. He grabbed some chopsticks and began to pry it off.

*OK, I'm dealing with a fool, but he's not the murderer.*

"Any other leads?" I asked.

The police chief shrugged. "We're looking into it. So far, nothing yet."

The "several leads" he had spoken of didn't amount to much. It was just him trying to sound efficient.

"So what's next?" I asked.

Grimal seemed at a loss and didn't answer for a moment. "Wait for the lab results to come back. Maybe the murderer left some trace in the vehicle. We're also digging into her past to check if there's anything there that might give a clue."

"Next of kin?"

"A sister in California. She's been notified. No husband or kids. She was single all her life. She took early retirement from—"

"State Parks and Recreation, I know. Why did she do that?"

Grimal looked annoyed at being interrupted

and by the fact that I knew what he was talking about already.

"She was an avid outdoorsy type," Grimal said. "She didn't like her job at Parks and Rec because she worked in the accounting office, in a cubicle where the only window in sight faced a parking lot. She always complained that she had joined the department to work in the great outdoors and never got a chance to. Her colleagues said she took early retirement so she could be outside all the time instead of just on weekends. Since she had no family to support, she could take the smaller retirement package."

"Any enemies at work?"

"None that I could find."

That meant nothing. "She ever uncover any stolen money while doing her accounting or steal any herself? Accountants often get sucked into crime or discover it."

Grimal paused for a second and then quickly said, "We're looking into that."

*You are now,* I thought with a smile.

"Did she ever do any accounting for the gym?" I asked.

"No, she was just a member. She volunteered to do the taxes at that resort, though."

"I see. That's interesting."

Grimal shook his head. "No it isn't. I called the IRS and the state tax people. They've never been under investigation except for a routine audit that they passed with flying colors."

*Maybe because they're good at hiding what they're doing,* I mused.

It was a thin lead, but it was the only one we had at the moment. And Grimal wouldn't be able to follow it by blundering around the offices of Sunnydale Nature Resort. If they really were cooking the books over there, Grimal's last visit had probably spooked them into burying the evidence even further.

So it was up to me. Great.

I'd let Grimal continue with the routine paper trail, something he was good enough at, and I'd have to do the undercover work. In a nudist colony.

I wished I had joined Suburban Fitness earlier.

At least it was a warm and sunny day in late spring as I drove out of town, headed for the first nudist colony I had ever stepped foot in. I had already sent an email to the director, Adrian Fletcher, saying I wanted to meet him and apply for membership. I'd read the website's extensive list of rules and found that you couldn't just show up, say hi, and bare all.

I drove a rental car just in case Adrian or

someone else I met that day was the murderer. Whoever I had chased had gotten a good look at my car, and I didn't want to announce myself by driving into the nudist colony with my own vehicle.

As I pulled off onto the leafy country lane leading to Sunnydale Nature Resort, I noticed my heart pounding in my chest at a rate unhealthy for anyone over fifty.

The resort lay at the end of a quiet gravel lane flanked by woods. I had seen no houses for the past mile. The lane was blocked by an automatic barrier, painted a bright red and equipped with reflectors so no unwary driver would slam into it. Above it was a large wooden sign about ten feet up stretching across the road and reading "Sunnydale Nature Resort" in letters carved into its surface.

To the side, I saw a small metal box on the top of a post. It had a camera, a button, and a little speaker. I pressed the button.

For a minute, no one answered, and I fought a strong temptation to turn around and drive back to town. Just as I put my hand on the gear shift to move into reverse, the speaker crackled to life.

"May I help you?" a man's voice asked. It would be a man, wouldn't it?

"It's, um, Barbara Gold. I have an appointment at the office."

"Oh, yes. Welcome to Sunnydale Nature Resort, Barbara. Drive up the road about half a mile and you'll see the office building on the left."

The speaker emitted a beep, and the barrier rose. I put the car back into drive and moved forward.

"Well, you certainly got yourself into it now, Barbara," I whispered to myself.

After about a hundred yards, the woods opened up into a wide field of grass speckled with wildflowers. Far to my right, a pond glittered in the sunlight. Nude figures cavorted by the side of the water or swam in the pond. My eyes bugged out, and I nearly drove off the road. I am not a prude, but I had never seen anything like this before, even from a distance.

I tried to control my reactions. If I looked skittish, it might make people suspicious.

Driving up a gentle slope, I crested a ridge, and the rest of the camp came into view. To the left I saw a building tucked up against the tree line with a sign saying "Office" in front of it. Ahead, the road continued to a long, low building with a sign saying "Rec Center." I could glimpse the corner of a pool behind it. To my right was a tennis court, where a doubles game was going on. Both teams looked like couples, the men rather portly, the women a bit saggy around the edges, but not the Gothic ruin that I was turning into. Some more activity areas lay beyond the tennis courts, but I couldn't see them clearly.

I parked in front of the office just as a man in his early sixties came out the front door, stood on the porch, and waved at me. He was wearing clothes, thankfully.

I parked, took a deep breath, and got out. When I came up to the porch, he shook my hand.

"Barbara Gold? I'm Adrian Fletcher. Pleased to meet you." He spoke with the slow drawl of the Deep South.

"Hello. Um, nice day, isn't it?"

"A beautiful day for some fun in the sun. Come on inside and meet my wife."

Not the usual thing a man says to a woman when they're about to undress, but okay.

The wife turned out to be Zoe Fletcher, a roly-poly little woman in her fifties. She was already naked, or nude. I've never known the difference. Since I've been to many women's locker rooms, her appearance in the buff did not shock me, although it felt a bit odd seeing her sitting behind a desk tapping away on a computer. I noticed her webcam was covered. Smart precaution.

Adrian got me a coffee, and we all sat down to chat.

"So have you tried nudism before?" Zoe asked. She spoke like she came from New England.

"Um, no. But I used to skinny dip with my friends when I was in high school. It felt so free, so natural. We'd sneak off to a lake deep in the woods where no one would see us and swim all day. We never told our parents. We'd bring our swimsuits along and dip them in the water before we headed back."

I made a good semblance of a laugh.

Adrian nodded and smiled. "A lot of nudists have stories like that."

I already knew that. I'd stolen that tale from a nudist website. I'd never been skinny dipping.

"So you'd like to recapture that feeling, eh?" Zoe asked. "That's great. You'll have a lot of fun here. Did you want an individual membership or a family membership?"

"Oh, my husband has passed."

*And is currently spinning in his grave, laughing hysterically.*

"What about your children and grandchildren?"

"I don't think they'd be interested."

"We have plenty of activities for kids."

I'd read that and wasn't sure how I felt about it.

It was beside the point anyway. I was here on a murder investigation.

The half-naked couple explained the rules of the place, which thankfully included a ban on photography, and went through the activities they had. It did seem like a nice resort with plenty to do, and they stressed that there were lots of seniors, including "one fellow who has been baring it all since he got back from World War Two." I love a man in uniform. Apparently I'd never see his.

"So would you like to check out the facilities and meet some of the members?" Zoe asked.

"Sure," I said with as much enthusiasm as I could muster.

"Great! Well, you'll have to take your clothes off. It's a clothing-free facility. There's a changing room back there with a locker. Take the key with you. It has a strap to go around your wrist."

Zoe led me to the room. As we left, I noticed Adrian pulling off his pants.

I thanked her, tried not to look at her husband (briefs, not boxers, a bad choice for him) and closed myself into the changing room.

The room was small, little more than a closet, with a few lockers and a full-length mirror on one wall.

I looked at myself in the mirror, really looked at

myself. It wasn't something I had done in a long time. I'd been in good physical health for most of my life and, I'm proud to say, pretty good looking. When I was younger, I had no shortage of suitors, especially from men who liked athletic women— soldiers, mercenaries, professional assassins, those sorts of people.

That had been a long time ago, and I had aged. Nothing wrong with that, it happens to everyone. Considering my lifestyle, making it to seventy was tantamount to winning the lottery. I had nothing to complain about.

But just *look at me*. I had put on some fat. My hair had gone gray. My hands looked like parchment. I had wrinkles on my face. I had wrinkles everywhere else too. I sagged in places that had once been springy and buoyant. Somehow going out with Octavian hadn't made me self-conscious. He just wanted some company like I did, along with some flirting that barely rose above the schoolyard level. A peck on the cheek was all I gave him and all he expected.

This was different. I was going to bare all in front of strangers.

And yet I had to. Someone had been murdered. The murderer had tried to kill me, too, and would try again if they knew who I was. They had tried to kill Pearl as well. It didn't matter that she had one foot in the grave and the other on a banana peel; she was my friend and deserved to be safe.

I took a deep breath and a final look in the mirror and started to undress.

# SIX

We walked out of the office—Adrian, Zoe and I—in our birthday suits. And boy, those birthdays were a long time ago. To avoid looking at Adrian, I spoke mostly with Zoe. It was surreal seeing her naked by my side while walking across a field in the sunlight, but the fact that she was a woman made it much easier.

Only in a relative sense. I was tense, mortified. Here I was on the wrong side of seventy walking naked in broad daylight. I didn't even walk naked at home. A trip from the shower to my bedroom was always done with a towel wrapped around me. Now my muscles tensed, and my hands tried to cover everything at once. I wanted to curl in on myself and had to force my body to take up a normal walking posture. If I didn't fit in here, I'd never be able to solve the murder.

"Let's go to the activity center first," Adrian suggested.

"All right," I replied, automatically turning to him as I spoke to him. Common courtesy, except that it made me see him. All of him. I did a good job maintaining eye contact. What unsettled me the most was how he was looking at me openly, unashamedly. He wasn't staring or ogling, but he was seeing all of me. I felt myself flush.

We headed up to the other building. Through a large window, I could see a young couple in their thirties, still relatively unlined and bouncy, playing Ping Pong. They laughed and joked like nothing was different about what they were doing than what I did at the park on weekends with my grandson.

Of greater interest was a notice board out front. Tacked on it, among other announcements, was the newspaper story about Clarissa Monell.

I feigned shock.

"Oh dear. I heard about this. She went to my gym."

"Yes, what a tragedy!" Zoe said. "She was a beloved member. Clarissa came here for many years. Volunteered with a lot of activities around the resort and for the past couple of years was our volunteer coordinator. She worked as an accountant and did our taxes for free."

"Helped us out quite a bit with that," Adrian put in.

They gave each other a significant look—Zoe accusatory, Adrian apologetic. Had the naked man revealed too much?

I realized I was staring at Adrian again, felt myself flush, and turned away.

To cover up my embarrassment, I asked, "So the two of you own this place?"

"Yep. Bought it twenty-one years ago," Zoe said, putting an arm around her husband. That brought him into my line of sight, and I turned to read the other notices on the board. There was a hike scheduled for tomorrow, plus a cookout on the weekend. There was also a memorial service for Clarissa Monell scheduled for tomorrow evening.

Bingo. I needed to go to that.

"I need to check on something down by the lake," Adrian said, and headed off in the other direction.

Fine by me. That took some of the pressure off, plus it gave me a chance to question Zoe alone.

She led me into the activity room. Several people played cards, Ping Pong, chess, and shuffleboard. They were of all ages from late twenties to people as old as I was.

Zoe introduced me to everyone. It was agonizing. I felt tense, exposed, and couldn't quite figure out where to direct my gaze. I decided eye contact was the safest, but if the conversation lasted more than a few seconds, it felt like I was trying to stare the other person down. The worst of it all was that I could see myself behaving awkwardly. The fact that everyone else acted so nonchalant made it worse. I stood out like a sore thumb.

"I'm surprised there are so many people here on a weekday," I said as we walked around the pool behind the rec center. A couple of people lay sunning themselves, all of themselves, while some more frolicked in the water.

"The retirees who live in the area come most every day when the weather is good. Others take the day off from work or come on their lunch break. There's nothing like taking an hour off in the middle of a busy work week and eating a bag lunch down at the lake."

"I see."

"Oh, wait until you see the crowd on the weekends. All the families come, as well as the younger people who can't get away from work."

"So kids don't have a problem with this?"

I couldn't believe I asked that, because it came out as a challenge. I was trying to fit in, lie low. This didn't help. It just came out, though.

Zoe didn't seem offended at all.

"Oh, kids are some of our most avid members," she said in a way that made it sound like she answered that question a lot. "You mentioned you raised children, so you know how hard it is to keep them in clothing. Come bath time, they're running all over the house naked, happy to be free of clothes. It's the same here."

I had a flashback to six-year-old Frederick doing just that. Innocent silliness, and in the privacy of our home.

"Aren't the parents worried, about, um …"

Zoe got serious. "Predators? We keep a close eye on all the children and encourage the parents to do the same. Any single male who wants to sign up must have a background check."

"That's good."

"Let's go down to the lake. I think you'll like it," my hostess suggested.

Oh great, and see Adrian again. Well, I'd seen plenty of naked men in the past twenty minutes. The problem with Adrian was that he was chatty and knew my name and email address.

As we were about to leave, I spotted another

noticeboard. It was quite large and covered with clippings from newspapers and magazines. I went over and saw all the articles were about nudism, and all were written by Adrian Fletcher.

"My husband has been an outspoken advocate for our lifestyle all his life. This is barely a tenth of what he's written."

"Adrian is amazing," a man said without looking up from his chess game.

"A real leader," another said. Everyone within earshot nodded.

"Shall we go down to the lake now?" Zoe asked.

*Let's not and say we did,* I thought. Instead, I let myself be led out of the activity building.

"You'll get used to it," Zoe said as we headed down the hill.

"Oh, I'm all right."

She shook her head and smiled. "You're nervous. It's perfectly natural. You'll get over it quickly enough. I bet you're already more relaxed than when you first took your clothes off, aren't you?"

I thought about it for a moment and had to concede that was true.

"It's strange," I said. "Walking with you here isn't so bad, even if we are out in the middle of a field. Being around the men is a bit uncomfortable, though."

*More than a bit,* I added silently.

Zoe looked at me slyly. "I bet if I were a gorgeous twenty-something, you'd feel uncomfortable too."

"You're quite good looking."

Zoe laughed. "I am to my husband, not to the rest of society. I'm short and overweight. But so what? I've always been like this. It's my natural body shape. I used to worry about it constantly, go on fad diets and exercise myself to exhaustion. I was always comparing myself to other women, even after I married Adrian. He adores me, but I didn't adore myself. Now I love my body."

"What changed?"

"Nudism. When you come out to a place like this, you notice that everyone has lumps and bumps and weird scars or body parts that are too small or too big. You stop worrying about it. After a while, you don't even really see it."

I didn't have a response to that. I couldn't decide whether she really meant it or was trying to fool herself. All this seemed so strange, and more than a bit artificial. I simply couldn't believe that these people were all wandering around naked and not getting some sort of sexual thrill out of it.

On the other hand, I saw young and old inter-acting more here than they did in the regular world. And I didn't see anyone gawking. Every woman develops a Gawking Sensor by age twelve, both for herself and for other women, and mine hadn't gone off since I'd gotten here.

We came to the lakeshore. It was a small lake fed by a little creek. A pier jutted out into the water. A woman dove off the end and swam away from us with powerful strokes. A few others lounged around on beach towels spread out on the verdant grass.

Adrian stood talking to one of the sunbathers, hands on hips, a scowl on his face. As soon as he saw us, his manner changed completely. He grinned and waved. The woman he'd been talking to got up and waded out into the water.

"This lake sure is lovely," I said. "I think this is my favorite place here."

While I was saying this, I kept an eye on Adrian. He glanced at the woman he had been speaking with, a flicker of annoyance passing over his features, then he composed himself and walked over to us.

"So what do you think?" he asked.

I faked a smile. "I think I'd like a year's membership."

"Great! Hey everyone, this is Barbara, and she's our newest member."

Everyone turned to me. I felt like sinking through the ground, clothing myself in soil and grass.

"Hi, Barbara!" several people said at once.

People came over and shook my hand and introduced themselves. This was good, because I was getting to know potential suspects. This was bad, because I was suddenly touching naked people and they were touching me.

I'm really not a prude, but this was too much.

Zoe put her arm around my shoulder.

"You've committed even though you're nervous. That shows courage."

Oh, my little naked Zoe. If you only knew what things my courage has accomplished.

And yet, why was doing this so much more disturbing than taking fire from a group of hostiles? Once in El Salvador, I'd been caught out in the open, paddling down a river in a canoe, when a group of rebels hidden in the jungle on the shore started firing at me. I was certainly more exposed then than I was now.

But in a way I wasn't. There's a certain honesty to war. Those rebels were quite clear in their intentions, and my rocket-propelled grenade quickly informed them of my own intentions. Here, on the other hand, I couldn't read the signals. I didn't know what these people's motivations were. Why would a middle-aged businessman leave work early to take off his clothes and romp around the countryside with people of all ages? Why would a married couple in their sixties do the same? And why, on God's green Earth, would people bring their children to such a place?

I believed Zoe's utopian ideas to a point. People did seem comfortable with their bodies here, even people as old as me. This wasn't a sex club. There was no shortage of those in the city. And this wasn't about seeing naked children; otherwise no one would be here on a school day. This was something different, something more subtle. What, I wasn't quite sure.

But I got the feeling that if I figured that out, I might get closer to solving Clarissa's murder.

I left Sunnydale Nature Resort with a mixture of relief and confusion. My purse was stuffed with promotional material about the resort and the nudist movement in general. And it was a movement. There were several national organizations and a few hundred nudist resorts, campgrounds, and hotels across the country. I had pamphlets titled "The ABCs of Nudism," "Nudism for all Ages," and "Political Naturism: How We Can Bring Peace to the World Through a Clothing-Free Lifestyle."

The last one was my favorite. Imagine telling an Islamist terrorist that if he took his clothes off, he wouldn't have to blow himself up! I guessed that was true to a point. A suicide vest counts as clothing, after all.

My next step was to read all this stuff and do some more Internet research before I went to the memorial service. My membership got me onto an online forum for Sunnydale Nature Resort. That could prove useful.

I had to stop by the supermarket before going back home to get some laundry detergent, which I had forgotten on my last shopping trip because of the excitement of seeing the murder, and then visit Pearl to make sure she didn't need anything. That got me locked into a two-hour conversation about nothing in particular, and so when I finally got back home, the sun had set and my front porch was dark.

As soon as I pulled into the driveway, parked my rental car behind my own car, and switched off the engine, I knew something was wrong.

## SEVEN

Over the years, I'd developed a gut instinct for danger. It had saved my life more times than I could count, and I'd learn to respect this feeling.

So I ducked beneath the dashboard and pulled the pepper spray from my purse. My 9mm automatic was in my bedside table in the house, as dangerous as a feather duster for all the good it would do me right now.

For half a minute, I stayed where I was, ears perked. I heard nothing. I heard the wind through the leaves, the annoying yap-yap dog next door barking incessantly, the engine of a distant car, the faint sound of a television in one of the neighboring houses, but nothing important. My mind spun into overdrive, trying to figure out what had jerked me into this hyperawareness.

I got out the passenger side, just to be unpredictable, and kept low as I gripped my pepper spray and moved to the door.

Then I noticed what had set the warning bells off. It was my welcome mat. The mat was poorly made. The Chinese factory had made the bottom too slick, and it kept slipping away from the door. Why anyone would put a slick bottom on a welcome mat is beyond me. Things just aren't made as well as they used to be. I'd been meaning to replace it because it was a nuisance having to push it flush against the door again every time I stepped on it and dislodged it. I distinctly remembered it sliding beneath my feet as I left the house to go to the nudist camp. I remembered saying, "Barbara, if you don't change this welcome mat it's going to be the death of you."

Now it was dislodged again, lying at an angle with one corner a good two inches from the door. I had put it back in its place this afternoon. I'd bet my life on it.

Someone had been here.

I didn't subscribe to the newspaper, and my mailbox was by the sidewalk. There was no reason for someone to come onto my porch.

No friendly reason, anyway.

I checked my phone. My house was equipped

with a state-of-the-art burglar alarm that sent a notification to my phone if it got set off. I'd installed it after being visited by a professional assassin. I'd clubbed him with a can of hairspray and sent him on his way.

But that's another story.

My phone informed me that I hadn't received a notification. So someone had come onto my porch but hadn't broken in, or had broken in and was enough of a pro to disable the alarm. I was either safe or in a whole mess of danger.

I used the flashlight app on my phone to examine the door. It hadn't been broken open. There were no telltale marks near the lock. Had it been picked?

Gently I tried the door and found it still locked. Then a gleam in the flashlight beam caught my eye. Something was stuck in my lock.

I took a closer look and saw only a fuzzy haze. I'd left my reading glasses in the car. Frustrated, I took a photo of the lock and zoomed in on the image.

The end of a metal wire, what looked like part of a paperclip, stuck out of my lock. I tried to pull it out with my fingertips and found it was too lodged in there to budge.

So I was dealing with an amateur. Opening a

lock with a paperclip only works in the movies. Feeling more confident, I moved to my back door and unlocked it, keeping my pepper spray at the ready. Amateurs could be deadly too.

Getting through the back door, I left the lights off and hurried to the bedroom, eyes sharp for any movement in the shadows. The burglar alarm sensed the door opening and started beeping, warning me I had sixty seconds to punch in the code before it sent a warning to the company. I ignored it. As soon as I got to my bedside table, I pulled out my 9mm, flicked off the safety, and felt much better.

Just then something moved in the hallway. I brought my gun level, ready to fire, and then relaxed. Dandelion scurried out of the darkness and attached herself to my leg. Nothing like four sets of tiny claws digging into your flesh to tell you that you're home.

The alarm started beeping louder and at shorter intervals, warning me my time was running out.

Shaking Dandelion off my leg and ruining my pantyhose in the process, I made a thorough search of the house and found no sign that anyone had broken in. I was just about finished with my search when my alarm gave a long, sustained beep. My time had run out. I continued to ignore it until I finished my search. Then I went to the alarm, punched in the code, and stopped its annoying noise.

My cell phone started ringing, its sound muffled inside my purse, which I had left on the back porch. I went over and answered.

It was the alarm company.

"Mrs. Gold? This is Sentinel Alarm," a concerned woman's voice told me. "We detected your burglar alarm going off in your house two minutes ago."

I put on my sweet little old lady voice. "Oh, I do apologize. I'm here, and everything's fine. It was my cat."

"Your cat set off the burglar alarm?"

"Um, well, not exactly. You see, Dandelion grabbed at my leg when I came through the door and distracted me. Cats can be such a distraction, can't they?"

"Whatever you say, Mrs. Gold. Would you like us to set the timer for longer than sixty seconds to give you more time when coming through the door? We do that with many of our customers who have mobility issues."

It's amazing how quickly people become condescending when they notice you're old.

"Oh, that's quite all right. By the way, was the

alarm turned off at any time between one in the afternoon and now?"

I could hear her tapping the keyboard on the other end of the line.

"No, ma'am. Did you expect someone to come into your house?" The poor woman on the other end of the phone sounded confused. "If you have memory issues, we can assign a customer service representative to help you with your security needs."

We'd moved from mobility issues to memory issues? She'd also started speaking more loudly and slowly.

Time for a counterattack.

"Oh, no memory issues. I was just wondering if my grandson stopped by to visit while I was at the nudist colony."

Dead silence. I grinned.

"Anyway," I continued, "thank you for calling. Most kind of you."

I hung up.

My next call was to Arnold Grimal, who was just about to leave the office after a hard day of paperwork and Chinese takeaway. I told him about the attempted break-in, and he said he'd send over an officer.

"Find out anything interesting today?" I asked.

"I spoke with the IRS again. No trouble with any of the tax returns for the resort. At my request, they had one of their experts take a look at their returns going back several years and found nothing suspicious."

"That's disappointing."

"Yeah, and I had a look at her will. She gave everything to several different environmental charities, except for a few family heirlooms that went to her sister. I also spoke with her physician. No history of mental illness or any serious physical problems. She was in good health for someone her age."

*Unlike you,* I thought. Yes, I can be catty at times.

"The doctor did tell me one interesting thing, though."

"Oh?"

"He prescribed her sleeping pills. She said she was under stress and couldn't sleep at night."

"Did she give a reason why?"

"No. Said it was personal."

"Hm."

"Hm, indeed. Oh, the autopsy didn't show drugs in her system beyond a trace amount of the sleeping pill, perfectly normal for someone the next morning after taking the prescribed dose. She was not abusing them. Didn't find any diseases or chronic conditions either."

And that was that. He had nothing more for me except a couple of pieces of a puzzle that still wasn't showing a coherent picture.

The officer arrived and checked the house and dusted for prints on the door. I didn't hold out much hope of finding prints since our murderer had been so careful with the stolen Lexus. The officer was very kind and said his chief had told him to stay to watch the house if I wanted him to. I declined. I'd probably be safer without the attentions of Cheerville's finest. Just to be on the safe side, I asked for a patrol car to pass by my house at regular intervals during the night. The officer assented to this request without a murmur, having no doubt been ordered by his police chief to do just that. Grimal knew if something happened to me, the CIA would have his head on a platter.

The policeman left, and I double-checked the house was secure, that all doors and windows were locked and the porch lights both in front and out back were on.

So the murderer had found my address. That gave me another clue about him or her. They had obviously noted my license plate number while I was noting the one on the Lexus and had access to the Department of Motor Vehicle files.

That meant either a DMV worker, a cop, or someone who knew a DMV worker or cop and could get them to look up my license plate.

I suspected it wasn't a cop who had come to my house. Even Cheerville's bumbling officers could pick a lock with more finesse than the person who had broken a paperclip in my front door. Plus, they would have noted the burglar alarm. So more likely a state employee. Perhaps someone at Parks and Rec? I didn't have any excuse to go over there, though.

I'd have to leave that part of the investigation to Grimal. I sent him a text outlining my suspicions and asking him to get a warrant to check the membership list and crosscheck it against anyone who could access the DMV files. Getting the warrant from the judge could be handled quickly enough, but I asked him to hold off on serving the warrant for the moment. I wanted another chance to tease out the truth myself. This murderer was an amateur but clever. If cops showed up at the nudist colony and started rifling through files, the murderer would be on their guard and could start thinking up an alibi and hiding evidence. It was better to catch them by surprise before that happened.

Grimal texted back that he'd "take care of everything." That did not make me feel better.

What made me feel even worse was the prickly feeling I was getting under my clothing. Had I sat down on any poison ivy at the nudist colony? Actually, it felt like I'd rolled in a whole patch of it.

I took off my clothes, out of sight of any crowd of strangers this time, and examined myself.

Oh dear. I had a sunburn in all the wrong places.

I glopped on a liberal amount of moisturizer and put on my nightgown. The material clung to me and made me even itchier, so I caved in to the inevitable, removed my nightie, and got into bed nude. It felt more comfortable.

Despite the attempted break-in, I slept well, secure in the knowledge that I had a good alarm system and anyone breaking in would be faced with a naked senior citizen with a gun in one hand, a can of pepper spray in the other, and a really bad temper after what she'd been through that day.

It was doubtful the intruder would come back in any case. This person was not stupid, just inexperienced. They knew I'd discover that bit of paperclip in my front door. Even if I hadn't seen it, I'd have noticed it when I tried to put my key in the lock. They would try to find another way to get me. Whoever it was, they were cold-blooded and methodical. I'd have to ask Grimal to keep an eye out for any more stolen cars in the area. Since the first murder had worked so well, the killer might try the same method on me.

What really worried me was the possibility that the killer was also a member of the nudist colony and had learned what I looked like. If they had seen the DMV scan of my driver's license, they'd know my face. My precaution with the rental car had achieved nothing. If they really did know what I looked like, they could come at me when I was vulnerable. There was no way to hide my 9mm in my towel, and carrying my purse around with me everywhere I went at Sunnydale would look suspicious.

Whatever happened at the nudist colony the next day, I would have to make sure that I was never out of sight of other people. I'd have to stick with the crowd. The killer wouldn't dare try anything against me then.

Not unless there was a grand conspiracy of nudists to take out Clarissa and all other opposition.

But that would be too weird even for Cheerville. Wouldn't it?

# EIGHT

The next day, I arrived at Sunnydale Nature Resort bright and early. I needed time to get to know people before the memorial service, which would be at seven that night. The air was muggy and carried the heat of early summer.

I still drove the rental, figuring that while I was on the road, it might keep the killer from recognizing me. Of course, if the killer really was at the nudist colony, they would know it was my car if they saw me getting out of it. So it wasn't much of an extra precaution, but in my line of work, I'd learned that even tiny added layers of safety could make a vital difference.

I had taken another precaution as well. This time I came armed with a large bottle of sunscreen with an SPF of a hundred. I hadn't known it came that high. It was called Sun Shield but should have been called Nudist's Necessity. I parked in front of the office and undressed in the car.

Adrian came out. He was nude this time, and from his appearance, I could tell the air conditioning was on inside. Adrian didn't seem the least bit embarrassed by this natural reaction of male anatomy, proving that he practiced what he preached about body positivity.

As I came out of the car, he stared at my body. No one had done that here before. In fact, no one had done that since my husband passed. I couldn't decide if I wanted to slap him, run away screaming, or curl up and die.

"Oh dear, I see you've made the first mistake of a new nudist," Adrian said.

"I look like a lobster whose face and hands somehow escaped the pot," I replied, somewhat relieved that he was looking at my body for a valid reason.

He chuckled. "Don't worry, sunburns are an occupational hazard in our lifestyle. Your skin will soon adjust, and you'll have a beautiful all-body tan."

He spoke the truth. Everyone else here was universally golden.

"I brought some suntan lotion this time," I said.

"Good. There's a brand called Sun Shield that has an SPF of a hundred."

"That's what I got."

"Smart woman. So what did you do before you retired?"

The suddenness and direct tone of the question took me aback. My cover story came out quickly enough, though. I'd had decades of practice.

"I was in the Foreign Service, working on development projects in the Middle East and Latin America."

"Government work, eh?" He did not look happy. "Well, enjoy your day."

He went back inside. I decided to head to the lake. As I ambled down the slope, I felt like I was being watched, like eyes were boring into my back. I peeked over my shoulder.

Adrian stood inside the open door to the office building, half obscured and no doubt thinking the relative shadow hid him from view.

He was looking right at me.

I pretended I hadn't noticed and continued my walk down to the lake.

Several people lay on the grass by the water or waded around in the shallows, thankfully all women. Most were of retirement age, except for one lovely girl who looked like she was in college.

She had a model's body and flawless skin. She stood waist deep in the water and was playfully splashing an older woman who resembled her enough that I guessed she was her mother.

Everyone greeted me in a friendly way, and I put my towel down next to the oldest woman there, someone about my age. I didn't notice my choice in companions until I had actually lain down. I'd chosen her automatically. Somehow I felt better sitting next to her.

That feeling disappeared as the young woman came out of the water toward me. The words Zoe had said came back to me.

*I bet if I were a gorgeous twenty-something, you'd feel uncomfortable.*

"Hi!" she said. "I'm Angie."

"Hello. I'm Barbara…" My voice trailed off as I noticed an ugly scar on her hip, several furrows that ran from the top of her hip to her thigh. Her right arm had some too. I hadn't noticed those at first because she had been partially turned away from me.

"Motorcycle accident," she said.

"Oh dear! I didn't mean to stare. I'm ever so sorry." What was the matter with me?

"It's all right. Our scars show our history. It's part of who we are."

She recited that line like some people recite the Scriptures.

"Well, I have plenty of scars too," I said, "although you probably can't tell through all the wrinkles."

"Wrinkles show our history too. They show someone has survived in the world and learned wisdom on the way."

"I'm not sure how much wisdom I have, but I certainly have the wrinkles."

I've never liked proselytizers. I respect people who have faith, and I have my own, but flaunting it has always struck me as going against the spirit of faith. It appeared that nudism was a religion with this girl, and she wanted to preach to a new convert.

She smiled. "You have the wisdom to try something new at your age."

"New? Oh yes, the sunburn. My grandson would call that a n00b move."

That means "newbie" and yes, it's spelled with two zeroes. Don't ask me why.

"You should bring him here," she said with a serene smile lighting up her face.

*I don't think so,* I thought. *Seeing you might bring on early puberty.*

She studied my body as if reading a textbook. I tensed under the scrutiny.

"What's that?" she asked, pointing. I looked at where she indicated and couldn't help but let out a little gasp. On my side, a couple of inches to the left of and a little below my belly button, was a bullet wound I'd received in the Sinai.

I hadn't even thought about it. I'd had it for more than thirty years, and since it was always covered with clothing or a bathing suit, I'd never paid it much mind. Now it was visible for all to see.

"Oh, that was from an operation. Laparoscopic surgery," I said.

The young woman's brow furrowed. "And it left so much scar tissue?"

*Don't tell me I'm talking to a medical student here*, I thought.

"Oh, it was a long time ago when the procedure was still experimental."

Her eyes moved down to my upper thigh, where I had a second bullet wound, this one earned in El Salvador in that incident with the canoe. Sank my canoe and nearly sank me.

I fell silent, a lame explanation caught on my tongue, and waited for her to say something.

Instead she smiled at me, said, "Welcome to Sunnydale," and sat down by her mother.

If anyone else thought our conversation had been strange or my scars suspicious, they didn't give any indication. Everyone introduced themselves and made small talk.

Eventually the conversation turned to Clarissa's death.

Angie seemed the most upset by it.

"She was a true believer in what we're doing here," she said. "Some people just come here for fun or to get away from the stress in their lives. That's all right, I guess, but she really tried to help the movement."

"How so?" I asked, remembering that comment about helping with the taxes.

Actually, it had been Zoe who had first mentioned it and then got angry when her husband said Clarissa had been a great help. Strange.

"She did everything," a middle-aged woman named Kim said. "Whatever needed doing, whenever there was a call for volunteers, she was the first in line."

"Adrian really came to rely on her," Angie said. The way she said it, a bit pointedly, seemed to imply something. The slightest of frowns from a couple of the others hinted at that too.

"She was a good woman," Kim stated as if to cut off the conversation that might have come. "Such a shame she should be cut off from life by some drunk driver."

There was a pause. Angie nodded.

"If more people lived like us, things like that wouldn't happen," another woman stated. "Unhealthy living leads to unhealthy choices. You'd never catch one of us driving drunk."

*But I would catch one of you trying to drive me off the road,* I thought. Out loud I asked Angie, "Is that how you had your accident? A drunk driver?"

Angie let out a little laugh. "No, although I know plenty of bike riders with stories like that. No, I just took a corner too fast, hit some gravel, and got a bad case of road rash."

"That was before her championship," a woman in her forties named Liz said.

"I got more careful after the accident," Angie said with a grin.

"Championship?" I asked.

"She won first place in the Tristate Motorcycle Meetup for the three-mile obstacle course," Liz said.

"Congratulations," I said, and ticked her off my list of suspects. If Angie could win an obstacle course on a motorcycle, she could have driven that Lexus better than the murderer had.

"So how many members does Sunnydale have?" I asked.

"Oh, several hundred. I'm not sure exactly," Liz said. The others shrugged.

Great. One down, several hundred to go.

My phone rang. Octavian. Suddenly I was acutely aware of where I was and the state I was in. I'd forgotten about it for a few minutes speaking with the ladies.

I felt tempted not to answer. Something about talking on the phone with my new boyfriend while in the buff made me horribly embarrassed.

The phone kept ringing. I really should start putting the darn thing on silent.

"Aren't you going to answer that?" Liz asked.

I walked away from the others and answered. Octavian's cheerful baritone came on the line.

"Hey, pretty lady, what are you up to today?"

"Oh, um, just enjoying the great outdoors," I said, flushing from head to toe and everywhere in between. I found myself putting my thumb over the phone's camera just in case it magically turned on somehow.

"Would you like some company?"

"Oh, um, I have a very busy schedule today, um, scheduling."

"Well, how about dinner tonight?"

"Oh, I really can't."

"Oh, that's all right," Octavian said in a way to show that it wasn't. "Maybe tomorrow?"

"Well, I'm taking care of Martin tomorrow night." Octavian had met Martin. Octavian had been friendly. Martin had been dismissive. "But if you're willing to brave a dinner at Fatberger, you're more than welcome to come along."

"Oh dear, I've heard of that place. I'll have to go back to seniors' yoga if I eat there."

"Oh, you're not going to yoga anymore?"

"No, I've taken up walking. Better to get out in the fresh air instead of gyrating in that Seniors' Center listening to joints crack."

"Hmm, I see what you mean." More likely, he had started going to the class to find someone. Now that he had, he saw no reason to go anymore. Quite flattering, I have to say.

"I'll call you tomorrow and we can arrange it," Octavian said. "Enjoy the sun. Make sure you don't get burned. The sun is strong today."

"You have no idea," I said as I rang off.

As I went back to the group, Liz smiled.

"Somebody's boyfriend doesn't know she's a nudist."

I stopped and stared.

"How did you know?" I asked.

"Because you didn't want to answer, and then

when you did, your face lit up. It was obviously someone you wanted to speak with, but you kept blushing and looking down at yourself. Don't worry, your secret is safe with us."

"Are you a private detective or something?" I asked as I sat down on my towel. That would be just my luck.

"No, I'm just observant. I used to be in the military, years back now, and I was trained to notice things. I was a forward observer for artillery."

I couldn't say for sure, but I swore she glanced at my bullet wound as she said this.

I gave her a mock salute, making sure I did it wrong. "Glad to meet you, General. Thank you for your service."

Liz laughed. "More like first lieutenant, but thanks for the promotion."

"Where were you stationed?"

"Germany for most of my service. I was in Operation Iraqi Freedom, though. Spent a year in the country after we took it."

"Tough stuff," I said, and ticked her off my list. If that woman had had to deal with the combat zones of Baghdad or Karbala, she would have been much more aggressive in trying to run me off the road. She would have also been more careful trying to break into my house. Not that the Army instructs the average soldier on how to perform combat driving or pick a lock, but she would have had enough situational awareness that she wouldn't have made the simple, silly mistakes the murderer had.

Unfortunately, her combat experience probably had educated her in what the scar from a bullet wound looked like. While she hadn't said anything, Liz almost certainly knew that I had been shot. She must be wondering about that. I hoped she wouldn't start wondering out loud.

"Good morning, ladies!" Two middle-aged men came sauntering down the slope toward the lake. I immediately felt self-conscious and grabbed my towel. I realized my mistake and put my towel back down. I really needed to get better at this if I was going to blend in.

It was the suddenness of their appearance. I'd been enjoying the sun and conversation with a group of women, and other than my telltale scars, I had stopped being self-conscious about being naked. Now all the old doubts and awkwardness came back.

They came back even more when the two came right up to me.

"You're new. Pleased to meet you," one rather handsome man in his fifties said. "I'm Charles. This is Brad."

"I'm Barbara," I said.

"Welcome to Sunnydale," both men said at the same time. They sounded like Tweedledee and Tweedledum, except they weren't roly-poly twins but attractive men twenty years my junior. Somehow that made it harder to speak with them.

There followed a light conversation that would have been utterly unremarkable except for the fact that none of us was wearing anything. I winced every time they glanced at my body. Not that they stared or anything—nobody in this place stared—they just did the usual male checking-out thing. You know, looking you in the face as you talk, and then their eyes flick down for a second to look at your body. They'd been doing that since I was a teenager. The frequency had dropped off remarkably in the past twenty years, but it still happened. They certainly did it a lot more when they made up an excuse to speak with Angie. It was a habit with men, or an instinct, and no amount of "we are all the same in our bodies" nudist philosophy was going to change that.

I found it irritating me that they were looking at her so much. Searching out this feeling, I came across two truths—one revealing and the other embarrassing.

First, they weren't looking at her bare breasts

any more than regular men on the street would have looked at her clothed breasts. If anything, they did it less.

Second, I wasn't angry at the men for wanting to look at Angie. I was angry at them for looking at her more than they looked at me.

*I need to get out of here,* I thought.

"I think I've had enough sun," one of the women said. "I'm going up to the activity room to play some Ping Pong. Anyone care to join me?"

"All right," I said, a bit too hastily.

The two men were already in the water. I breathed a sigh of relief.

*Come on, Barbara,* I chided myself. *If you can't stand being around men in this place, how are you going to solve this murder?*

## NINE

The memorial service was held on a hilltop over-
looking the camp. A line of trees stood nearby, the
crickets already making their whirring evening
song.

A small pyre of wood had been set up, its
bottom fringed with kindling. To one side stood a
table with a buffet meal. Hanging from the edge of
the table were several poster boards showing images
of Clarissa.

Most of them had been taken at the camp,
judging from the large amount of flesh tones I
could see from where I was standing. I made a
mental note to study those pictures when it came
time for the buffet.

Right now, I needed to study the crowd.

And it was an impressive one. At least a

hundred people had shown up and stood in a big circle around the pyre. They were of all ages, shapes, and sizes. Many looked somber. A couple cried softly. Others spoke in low tones among themselves. I tried to focus on their faces, imagining them as fully clothed bankers and secretaries and schoolteachers. It was a surreal experience, made more surreal when I recognized a few of them. Over there was the woman who ran the florist shop downtown. Not far away was the woman who gave out parking tickets to the tourists who came to see Cheerville's Colonial-era sights and inevitably parked in the wrong place. That young man standing nearly opposite me in the circle was the day manager at the supermarket I frequented. To my relief, he showed no sign of recognizing me.

One interesting detail I noticed was that the crowd lacked two things—besides clothing, that is.

The first was that there were virtually no racial minorities. I saw exactly one Hispanic couple and one black man. I suppose it wasn't so surprising that we were virtually all white, or at least golden thanks to the sun. Cheerville is an unusually white suburb, and I've heard that minorities can feel uncomfortable surrounded by a sea of white faces. Being surrounded by a sea of nude white bodies would probably only compound their discomfort.

GRANNY BARES IT ALL    91

I also noticed that there were only two teenagers, and they were the only ones wearing clothing. A boy about Martin's age wore a bathing suit and was staring at a girl aged around fifteen who wore a light wrap around her waist and chest. I saw several younger children, naked as if it were bath time, and even a couple of toddlers who really should have at least been wearing diapers, but the lack of teenagers was noticeable. Many of the adults were of the age where they would have had teenaged children, but they had stayed at home.

I'd read a bit about this on various nudist websites I'd studied. "Clothing-free" nudist camps often made an exception for kids in their teens, recognizing that the stage of life they were going through came with a lot of shyness and awkwardness about their developing bodies. This concession to their feelings showed sensitivity and more than a little practicality. I could just imagine some of the conversations that went on around a nudist family's dinner table.

"Mooom, do we have to go to a nudist camp again this year?"

"It's fun. Look at this brochure. There's a big swimming pool and tennis, and there's even horseback riding. Remember how much fun you had riding last year?"

"The saddle gave me blisters on my butt."

"Don't swear at the table."

"Sorry, Dad."

"You'll have a great time. And they say there's plenty of kids your age."

Kid blushes uncontrollably.

"Oh, and teens can wear clothing if they like."

"Really? Oh, that's cool. Can you show me that brochure? Hey, the pool looks great! And they have archery too. Can I do archery?"

The teenage years were a social status minefield. You tiptoed through several hazardous years trying to look cool and trying not to do anything embarrassing. A hard task under normal circumstances, even worse when one was expected to do it in the buff.

I had spent the day suppressing my own embarrassment and trying to chat with as many people as possible, ears perked for any mention of Clarissa Monell.

Not that I learned much. People said all the usual things about how she was a dedicated nudist and always lent a helping hand around the resort. Apparently she also wrote numerous articles for national nudist magazines, although under a pseudonym, since she didn't want to get in trouble at her government job.

So quite the activist, and well loved, at least on the surface. When someone dies, everyone tries to say their best about them. It's certainly not the time for complaining about the deceased's annoying habits or digging up some old personal rivalry. That would happen in private conversations I would not be privy to.

At quiet times during the day, I had used my phone to log into Sunnydale's online forum and found that Adrian was a bit of a naked celebrity. He'd done a lot of work for the movement, and everyone seemed to look up to and defer to him. Angie had especially sung his praises, and so had Liz and several of the others.

The memorial service was starting. Perhaps something interesting would be revealed here. Not the really juicy stuff, of course, but at this point in the investigation, I'd take what I could get.

Adrian and Zoe Fletcher stepped forward and stood close to the unlit pyre. Zoe addressed the crowd.

"We're here today to remember one of our own, one of our best. Clarissa Monell was known to all of you and loved by everyone. She was cut down in the prime of life by a horrible hit-and-run incident a couple of days ago."

I glanced around the circle, looking for guilty

faces, and saw none. Zoe's voice did not waver, and Adrian didn't look suspicious or tense. Either I couldn't see the murderer from where I stood, or the murderer had gotten their act together and put on a calm demeanor for the memorial service.

Zoe went on.

"I knew Clarissa for many years, and I always found her to be caring, giving, and honest."

Did I sense a slight stress on the word "honest"? I glanced at Adrian. His face was a mask.

"She was always a strong fighter for the nudist way of life and a helping hand to those in the community who needed her. Sadly, her work life was less than ideal. Like many of us, she was stuck in a stifling office, wrapped up in formal clothing, when she would rather be free to frolic through the fields as God had made her. I'm sure that many of you have memories of Clarissa that you'd like to share, so feel free to step forward and tell us all about them."

Someone stepped forward almost before Zoe finished her speech. I recognized the woman who Adrian had been speaking angrily to the first day I visited Sunnydale. She had swum away at our approach, and Adrian had put on a smile. I'd been wondering about her.

Zoe did not look terribly happy that she wanted to speak.

"Naomi, you wanted to say a few words?" the co-owner of the nudist colony asked, obviously wishing the answer would be "no."

"Yes, I would," Naomi said. She was in her forties but in good shape. A few stretch marks showed she had given birth. Otherwise she had healthy skin and toned muscles.

I stopped studying her body and listened to her words. Odd how I had never noticed other people's bodies as much as I did now. And here I was in the one place where bodies weren't supposed to matter.

"Like many of you, I only knew Clarissa through Sunnydale and a couple of regional conventions…"

Nudists have conventions? Like the Shriners? I imagined a bunch of old men wearing fezzes and nothing else driving around in little cars. That almost gave me the giggles.

*You're investigating a murder, Barbara. Focus.*

"…I always found her full of life and grace. She was a hard worker, too. As Adrian and Zoe know all too well, running a resort like this requires a lot of work. We have some great volunteers here to help them with that burden, but Clarissa was the best. She organized our volunteer program and made it run more smoothly. She also volunteered to manage the resort's taxes, something she did for free. Adrian and Zoe were kind enough to offer her free membership, but she wouldn't hear of taking any other payment…"

Adrian and Zoe had lost their poker faces. Adrian looked annoyed at Naomi. Zoe looked annoyed at Adrian.

And yet the IRS had confirmed that there was nothing amiss with the resort's tax returns. Plus those returns showed the resort was solidly in the black. Sure, something could be hidden, but so far, Grimal and the IRS had found nothing.

So what was going on with those taxes?

"When Clarissa decided not to do the taxes anymore because of her failing health, she was kind enough to teach me how to do it."

This set off a big red flashing light in my head. Clarissa did not have failing health. She had had a checkup just a few months before she died, and she was in remarkable health. Had she lied? It seemed an unlikely lie to expect anyone to believe. If she was swimming and playing tennis naked in front of the whole community, it would be hard for them to believe she was ill.

Perhaps she simply gave that excuse hoping no one would challenge her on it. We all do that sometimes, tell unconvincing lies or half-truths knowing that most people, eager to avoid an argument, won't publicly doubt us.

I bet someone in this gathering knew the real reason she had quit. I bet several someones did.

"She was a great asset to the community, and it will be hard to fill her shoes, even though she was most comfortable not wearing them," Naomi concluded.

The joke fell flat. A few people smiled politely, but no one laughed, least of all Adrian.

He stepped forward.

"Thank you, Naomi," he said. "Yes, there are a lot of vacancies to fill now that Clarissa is gone. Luckily, two of the main ones are already filled. Naomi has taken over the taxes and is helping with the accounting, and Angie Dickson has graciously agreed to take over as volunteer coordinator."

"What?" Zoe gasped, looking outraged. I thought I heard a few others say the same. There was certainly no shortage of surprised and angry faces in that circle.

Adrian's words rolled right over them. "Angie has been with us for many years and has been a leading volunteer in all aspects of our community. She has also been active on the national and international levels and been to many regional and national meetups. I think she'll make a fine volunteer coordinator. Welcome to the team, Angie."

"I'm glad to be of service," Angie replied.

Her tone caught me off guard. I thought she'd be embarrassed by the sudden outburst of disapproval or defiance that she had gotten the position even though for some reason some people didn't want her in it. Instead, she was looking daggers at Adrian.

A man stepped forward without asking and gave his own testimony about Clarissa, which amounted to little more than platitudes about how nice she was and how much of an asset she had been to the community. That seemed to break the ice, and everyone remembered they were at a memorial service. A couple more people stepped forward after him and also gave anecdotes about Clarissa.

None of those amounted to much. I got the impression that most people liked Clarissa, that she truly was a popular figure, although just beneath the surface, there was some sort of bubbling tension involving her. People knew that there was trouble in Eden, although most people did not know the full, naked truth.

At last, a strapping young man brought forth a lit torch and set the pyre ablaze. The wood had been doused with lighter fluid, and the flames shot up. Within seconds, the pyre was steadily burning, the wood crackling and sending sparks high up into the night sky to mingle with the stars.

Someone announced that the buffet was open, and everyone lined up to get some food.

In front of me stood two middle-aged women with a small boy holding on to one of their hands.

"I can't believe he had the gall to name her as volunteer coordinator," she whispered.

"And she accepted!" the other replied.

"What's going on?" the boy asked.

"Nothing," his mother said. "Let's get some pie."

The two women gave each other a significant look. Sadly, the child's question had cut their conversation short.

Lining up for food gave me a chance to study the photos. Clarissa really had done everything around Sunnydale. There were photos of her teaching a crafts class for children, one of her cleaning the pool with an expression of mock horror, an eye-popping one of her leading a yoga class, and several of her simply hanging out in various spots around the resort with other nudists.

Those were significant. It was remarkable how many of those shots included Adrian. Virtually none of them included Zoe. The most telling shot was a row of sunbathers with their feet dipped in the lake. Adrian had his arm around Clarissa, who smiled awkwardly at the camera, while Zoe sat on the other side of Adrian, actually leaning slightly away from her husband.

*Well, well, well. Now we're getting somewhere.*

I glanced at Zoe, who had regained her demeanor and was chatting amiably with a small circle of men and women. Could this happy-go-lucky woman really run someone down with a car? And if Adrian was the philandering type, why not run him down?

I gathered my food and kept my eyes open and ears perked.

The buffet was lovely. Nudists turned out to be great cooks. With my lack of culinary ability, I hoped I wouldn't be invited to a potluck. I'm always the awkward one bringing a bag of chips or some supermarket muffins.

I mingled with the crowd, hoping to hear some more juicy gossip, but I had run out of luck. Everyone was either saying kind nothings about the recently deceased or not speaking at all. In fact, quite a few people were silent.

Once again, I was struck by how unusually normal all these people were. I'd been to more than my fair share of wakes and memorial services, both for people who had died in combat and for those who had died of old age. They were all more or less like this. The majority had only good things to say about the deceased, but always some of the tensions the person had created in life came to the surface once they had passed.

I remembered one memorial service for a Marine killed in Iraq that ended up in a brawl. Apparently the Marine's brother had been sleeping with another Marine's wife. The deceased had had nothing to do with it and probably didn't even know, but his dying had led to the fight because it brought the two other men into the same room. The stress of a combat loss had broken what reserve they had mustered, and soon they were in a no-holds-barred fistfight. Most unseemly. They both got demoted.

I circulated for some more time but found out nothing more. I did notice that Angie had left early.

I eventually left as well, coming away with more questions than answers.

Unfortunately, that meant that I'd have to come back to this crazy place the next day.

## TEN

When I got home, I found no sign of another attempted break-in, but shortly after I returned, there was a knock on the door.

Gripping my 9mm automatic, I went to the door and looked through the peephole.

A peephole has saved my life more times than I can count. I don't know why everyone doesn't have a peephole in their front door.

This time, however, I didn't see a potential intruder, only one of Cheerville's finest. I opened the door a crack, keeping my gun out of sight. No point getting him jumpy.

"Did Grimal order you to keep checking on my house?" I asked.

"Yes, ma'am," he said, touching his hat like he was in a Western movie. "Until this whole thing is cleared up. That's what I wanted to talk with you about. Just an hour ago, I noticed a pedestrian wearing a hooded sweatshirt, sweatpants, and running shoes jog by your house. I noted that he or she was unusually warmly dressed for such a warm evening and suspected they might be trying to hide their features. I circled around and spotted the jogger passing by your house again. I turned on my lights, and the suspect bolted."

"And got away."

The cop looked embarrassed, as well he should.

"Yes, ma'am."

I rolled my eyes like I was my thirteen-year-old grandson.

"We'll keep a sharp lookout for them," the police officer promised. "You'll be protected."

I rolled my eyes again to express my feelings about the value of his "protection."

"Can you at least give me a description?"

"Yellow sweatshirt, gray sweatpants, blue sneakers. No visible logos or writing. About five-eight or five-ten, medium build."

There was a pause.

"That's it?" I asked.

"Yes, ma'am."

I gave him the kind of stare I used to give raw

recruits when they thought they knew more than I did.

"Here's what you're going to do," I said. "You're going to call Grimal and tell him that I don't want police protection."

"But—"

I raised a hand. The guy actually flinched.

"You're going to go off and do whatever it is you do in this town. Go save a cat from a tree. Go give someone a parking ticket. Go home. Whatever. But you and your colleagues are not going to patrol around my house."

"But—"

"Call Grimal and tell him I said so."

I slammed the door in his face.

It took him five minutes to leave, but leave he did.

In the meantime, I checked all the windows and the back door and made sure my security was working all right. While I wanted my hooded friend to come back, I wanted to be prepared.

So whoever it was had come an hour ago. I did the math. After I left Sunnydale, I had stopped in to see Pearl to ask if she needed anything. She kept me for about an hour and a half, complaining about her nurse, who was in the same room, and nattering on about the state of the world in general. It turned out that she didn't need anything. I made a mental note to check with a call instead of a visit in the future. She had made me miss the murderer, or at least a prime suspect.

I smiled, thinking I was still young at heart. The old me (meaning the young me) had always felt cheated when she missed some of the action. That hadn't changed.

So who could this be? The officer said the person was five-eight to five-ten with a medium build. That could be a lot of people. It ruled out Zoe, but it could be Adrian or Naomi or any one of a dozen people I'd met. It could be none of them. It would take a lot of chutzpah to show up at the memorial service of someone you had just killed, although the killer was cold-blooded enough to consider it just to allay suspicion. I was almost as stuck as I had been before. Too many suspects, not enough information.

Which was why I'd told the cops to beat it.

I wanted to face the killer myself. The police would only get in the way.

After feeding Dandelion and making a pot of coffee, I turned off all the lights, opened the curtains facing the street half an inch, and settled down in a chair just behind them, expecting a long wait.

It turned out I only needed to wait two hours.

The street was silent when the hooded figure came. My neighborhood was a sleepy one, and few people walked around after dark, so the hooded jogger with the slow but steady pace going along the opposite side of the street stood out plain as day.

The figure passed by my house, disappeared from view, and doubled back a minute later.

I thought my mysterious visitor would come up to the front or back door and try to break in again, but instead, he or she hurried across the street and disappeared into the shade of a maple tree close to the house. No lights were on in the house, and the light from the nearest streetlamp left the space under the tree in deep shadow.

The figure did not reappear. There was nowhere for them to go. Behind that shadowed area was only the house and a stretch of garden blocked off by a trellis. So they were still in there, hunched down in the shadow, waiting.

So I waited too, somewhat confused. Was my visitor watching the house? Why? My lights were off, and no one else was on the street. Now was the perfect time to try to break in.

Whoever it was didn't seem to be in any hurry. Minutes stretched on. I sat perfectly still, my gun in one hand and my pepper spray in the other, sitting in my chair, staring at that blob of shadow on the opposite side of the street. After about twenty minutes of this, a car drove by, its headlights partially illuminating the area under the tree. In the couple of seconds of light, I could not make out my visitor. He or she could have been any one of a number of shadows and vague shapes.

He or she? Yes, I had a vague hunch that it might be a woman. Women's and men's hips are made differently, and when women run, their feet tend to splay out more. It had been difficult to see when the person had been running in the half darkness, but I had gotten the impression that I was dealing with a woman.

Another car passed, but still I could not spot the person watching the house. Had they slipped away somehow? I didn't think so.

Patience. If working in war zones teaches you anything, it's patience. Sometimes you just have to hunker down and wait. Getting nervous or antsy and making a move before the time is right can get your head blown off.

So I kept waiting.

Minutes turned into half an hour, then an hour.

Our mutual wait was approaching two hours when something unexpected happened.

A second jogger came down the street. Like the

first, this jogger wore a hooded sweatshirt, but the newcomer looked somewhat taller than the first. This second jogger came directly for my house.

What was this, a murderer's convention? I flicked the safety off my gun.

The figure that had been hiding under the tree appeared again, moving quickly and silently at the newcomer, who didn't notice.

A loud beep sounded from down the street, and suddenly everything was illuminated by spinning red and blue lights.

Both figures spun, saw the approaching police car, and bolted down the street.

"Darn it!"

I ran for the door. Well, "run" is a generous term, but I made for the door as quickly as I could. I could have killed Grimal. Just as things were getting interesting, he had to send one of his squad cars to mess everything up!

By the time I flung open my front door, the whole scene had changed. My two visitors had bolted in opposite directions, both opting to cut between the houses to get to adjoining streets. The squad car had roared off around the corner to try to cut one of them off. I went after the other one, the taller, first visitor, who I could just now see diving into the shadows between the houses of two of my neighbors.

This person was far quicker than me, so running them down was not an option. Instead I made an educated guess about which way they would go and tried to get in front of them.

Assuming my visitor had scouted out my neighborhood, they'd know that beyond those two houses lay another residential street. Taking a right on that street would get them to a larger, busier street, the one from which the police car had come. Going left would bring them to a dead end and a small park— an open stretch of grass with a few young trees mostly used by dog walkers and joggers. Not much cover there, but the police would have to pursue on foot.

That would be the smarter way to go. Of course, my visitor could always continue to the next street over but would be faced with the same choice. Continuing through the houses to the street after that would get them to a busy area with some shops and a lot more lights. Not a good choice.

So I angled to the left, cutting between some houses farther down the street and closer to the little park. I figured my target would be moving slowly for a time, hiding in the shadows and checking every direction for signs of pursuit. With some luck, I'd be able to get ahead of them.

My luck held, barely. I huffed down a dark space between two of my neighbors' houses, nearly killing myself on a tricycle little Billy Dawson had left out in the yard, and came within sight of the next street. Soft footsteps close to my right told me where my target was.

I crouched as much as my knees would allow and swung around the corner, leading with my gun.

"Freeze!" I shouted.

## ELEVEN

The next instant, I nearly fired. The hooded figure snaked a compact .38 automatic out of the pocket of their sweatshirt and nearly got it level before seeing my gun and stopping.

Wow. Nearly beat me to the draw even though I got the drop on them. Whoever this was, they were good.

"Drop the gun," I ordered. "You won't get yours up in time, and besides, mine's bigger."

The figure's head moved, and the streetlight illuminated the face.

Liz. The Gulf War veteran from Sunnydale Nature Resort.

She grinned. "Mine's bigger than yours? You're talking like a guy."

"No I'm not, because I'm actually talking about my gun."

Liz chuckled and dropped her gun on the grass. "I'm not the one you're looking for."

I cocked my head. "No. No, you're not."

She was too good. She would have thought of a better plan to kill Clarissa Monell than running her over in the middle of town, and she would have maneuvered the car better in the chase. And she certainly wouldn't have made the rookie move of trying to break into my house with a paperclip.

I motioned with my gun for her to back up and grabbed her piece from where it lay on the grass. The safety was on. Every soldier keeps their gun at the ready if they think they're going to get into a combat situation. Liz obviously felt that threatening with the gun would be sufficient.

"So what are you doing here?" I asked.

The house we stood by was suddenly silhouetted by flashing red and blue lights. The patrol car moved slowly down my street. Cheerville's brave public servants had let yet another suspect get away.

A light came on upstairs.

"Let's go," I whispered. I put a gun in either pocket.

"Where?" she asked.

"To explain to the Keystone Cops that they

aren't needed. They're going to wake up the whole neighborhood at this rate, and I don't like to be conspicuous. You walk ahead."

That last instruction was because I still didn't fully trust her. I wasn't sure what was going on. My gut told me she didn't pose a danger, but that didn't mean I had to run any unnecessary risks.

I flagged down the squad car. It was the same officer I'd dismissed before. I explained that Liz was my friend and had been watching my house for me, that the real culprit had run off, and that he'd better run off himself and try to find them.

As the squad car did a one-eighty, tires screeching, sirens wailing, thereby warning the murderer to hide, I made a call to Grimal. I'm happy to say I woke him up. Yes, I had his home number. The CIA is a handy ally when it comes to finding out that sort of thing. I told him what had happened. He sounded grumpy. Whether grumpy about being woken up or about the incompetence of his officer I couldn't say.

But I could guess.

Once the police were out of our hair, we got down to business.

I brought Liz home. Dandelion took one look at Liz and started clawing her leg.

"She likes you. Usually she hides under the

couch when strangers appear. Sit down and let's talk."

She detached herself from my kitten and took a seat on my sofa. I sat on the opposite side of the room and covered her with my gun. While she was younger and healthier, there was no way she could make it across the room and disarm me before I plugged her.

Somehow I didn't think that would be necessary. Liz wasn't a threat. Just what she was, I wasn't sure.

"All right," I said. "Get talking."

"I went to the dentist the other day, and he was talking all about the hit and run. He was there, and he told me things that didn't appear in the papers. From what the eyewitnesses told him, the car shot out of a parking space and deliberately hit her. He didn't see it himself, but that's what everyone was shouting about when he got to the scene. It was murder, not a hit and run."

"Why didn't you go to the police?" I asked.

"Because when that prettied-up version of events hit the papers, I knew the cops thought it was murder too and were investigating."

"If you can call it that," I grumbled. "Go on."

"There's been some tension at Sunnydale, and I wondered if someone there might have done it. Then you showed up. Someone with old bullet wounds joining the camp just after Clarissa got murdered? That couldn't be a coincidence. What are you, ex-SWAT or something?"

"Never mind me," I said, dismissing the question with a gesture of my gun. "Tell me more about the tensions at Sunnydale."

She shifted in her seat, looking uncomfortable. It took her some time to speak.

"I joined a few years ago, just after I got out of the Army. I loved my time in the service, but I desperately needed a change. All those regulations and the uniforms and even worse, the uniformity. I wanted to be free. So I turned to nudism. I'd always been interested in it. It seemed a good way to express myself."

"You talk like Angie."

Liz chuckled. "A true believer, to be sure. Nudism really is liberating, but she takes it too far. Almost makes a religion out of it."

"So tell me more about this tension."

Liz made a face like she'd tasted something sour. "Adrian."

"He had eyes for Clarissa?"

Liz looked confused. "What? No, he had eyes for Angie."

Well, that explained Zoe's anger at Adrian naming Angie volunteer coordinator. Angie had been angry at it too, so I guessed the attraction wasn't mutual. She hadn't declined the offer, though.

"So Adrian has been harassing her?"

"Nothing overt. No one would stand for that. But he's always coming around to talk with her, always getting her on the same projects he's working on. She's almost as big a volunteer as Clarissa was, so she was the obvious choice to take over as volunteer coordinator, except that she didn't ask for the job. It would mean Adrian would have more excuses to be near her."

"But she didn't refuse the job."

"At Clarissa's memorial service? She wouldn't do that. She respected Clarissa. I'm sure she'll tell Adrian where to go, just not in front of a whole group of people."

"When we were down by the lake, I sensed some tension between Angie and Clarissa. Some of the other women seemed to have disapproved of Clarissa too."

"More disapproval over Adrian and Clarissa's relationship."

"I thought Adrian wasn't interested in her."

"Not in that way. But he leaned on her like a crutch. She was so capable, so willing to help, that he foisted way too much work on her. He took advantage of her. Zoe said words to that effect on more than one occasion."

"Did she try to stop it?"

Liz gave a wry smile. "No. Like I said, she was invaluable. And it's hard to say no to Adrian. He's done so much for the movement that everyone respects him despite his flaws."

I remembered the doctor prescribing her sleeping pills. "Was Clarissa under any stress?"

"She always pushed herself hard. That was just her nature. She kept up a sunny disposition, though. If she was under any stress, her first instinct was to hide it. She was a 'life of the party' type. She was happiest when everyone was happy around her. Showing she was stressed would spoil the mood. So if she was, or if she felt threatened, she wouldn't have shown it."

I nodded. The life of the party was often the loneliest person in the room.

"So who would kill Clarissa?" I asked.

She shrugged. "Darned if I know. I was hoping to find out when I came here."

"How did you know where I live?"

"I followed you this afternoon."

My brow furrowed. "No you didn't. I kept checking my rearview mirror on those country roads. No one was behind me."

Liz smiled. "I was in front of you. When you said you were going to leave, I hurried out of there before you did. There's only one main road into town, the one that goes by that gas station by the old farmhouse. I parked there, waiting for you to pass. Then I followed you."

I groaned. By the time I'd made it that far, I'd felt confident I wasn't being tailed and had stopped paying attention. I'd been outmaneuvered.

"All right, but how did you know the murderer would come after me in my home?"

"A hunch. New members have to give their home address. That means Adrian and Zoe both know where you live. Plus there's no security at the office. They don't lock it during the day. If they're out and about, anyone could walk in there and read your membership form. I'm sure the murderer must have wondered about you the same as I did."

"Wonderful. For a second there I thought we had it narrowed down to Adrian or Zoe."

"I'm afraid not. My gut tells me it's neither of them. To be honest, while there's plenty of tension at Sunnydale, I can't think of any reason why it would lead to murder."

So the murderer hadn't needed to see my DMV file. He or she could have simply gotten my address off the membership form. And people didn't need to sign in when they came to Sunnydale. There was no record of who had been there at the same time I was.

This was getting more and more confusing.

"On my first day, I noticed some tension between Adrian and Naomi down at the lake. Know anything about that?"

Liz shrugged. "Not that I know of. Maybe she isn't doing the taxes as well as Clarissa did?"

I bit my lip. Liz wasn't being as helpful as I'd hoped.

So let's see. We had Adrian and Zoe exploiting Clarissa's generosity, with everyone disapproving but no one doing anything to stop it. Someone killed her, and Adrian got Naomi and Angie to fill her shoes. For some reason he got angry at Naomi.

Oh, and Adrian was interested in the most beautiful woman in the resort. Typical. A middle-aged man hitting on Angie looked worse in the nudist context. That culture tried to make being nude something that wasn't sexual, and Adrian was showing that up to be a lie. Or at least a lie in his case.

I still didn't have a cause for murder, however. I needed to speak with Angie and Zoe and Naomi. Just how I would go about that would require some thinking.

That would all have to wait. Family had inter-vened, and I had to babysit Martin from right after he got out of school until late in the evening. I wouldn't have time to go to Sunnydale. It was frustrating to be so close and lose a whole day, but I couldn't see a way out of it. Pulling back might be a good thing, though. If I went three days in a row as a new member, that would raise some eyebrows.

With the attempted break-in, I had to come up with an excuse not to have Martin sleep over, claiming that I had to pick up Pearl first thing in the morning. That kept Martin from complaining. Usually he liked staying at my place because he got to play with Dandelion, but the mention of Pearl kept him away. He always claimed she smelled funny.

To be honest, I was glad to have a break from all this naked insanity.

"So now what?" Liz asked.

I had been silent for a time.

"I can't come to Sunnydale tomorrow. Family commitments. Can you go tomorrow?"

"Yes. I'm between jobs at the moment. What would you like me to do?"

"Keep an eye on everyone. Listen in on any conversation you can about Angie and Naomi and their new jobs. Also try and find out what the others think of me."

"I can do that."

I stood up. "Glad to have you aboard."

She extended her hand. I crossed the room and shook it. When I pulled my hand away, she kept hers extended.

"May I have my gun back?" she asked.

I handed it to her and turned away. As I did so, I put my own gun in my waistband.

"Glad to have you aboard," I repeated to mask the sound of my flicking off the safety.

I kept my back to her and took a couple of steps away as if I was going to sit back in my chair. On the mantelpiece behind the chair was a framed photo of myself and my late husband. It had been taken at a beach at night. Only ourselves and a bit of sand at our feet was illuminated, the background black in contrast to the flash of the camera. The combination of the dark background and glass covering made the photo a good mirror. I watched Liz's every move.

She checked her gun like a good soldier, making sure the safety was on and the gun was clean.

Liz glanced up at me, and I tensed. Had I been wrong to put my faith in her?

I got ready to draw, spin, and crouch at the

same time. I'd mastered that move in my youth, but I hadn't used it in years.

Turned out I didn't have to. A moment later, Liz put the gun in the pocket of her sweatshirt.

All that had taken less than four seconds. I turned, smiled at her, and bid her goodnight.

I had an ally. Now all I needed was some solid leads.

## TWELVE

Fatberger's decor lived up to its name. In addition to the smiling Fatberger character, there were large photographs of actual fatbergs taken in the United Kingdom's sewer system.

They were horrible to look upon. These massive chunks of slime, glistening a sickly white in the headlamps of Her Majesty's sewer workers, looked strangely like the pot bellies I'd seen on some of the men at the nudist colony. One poster was adorned with a gold banner saying "Fatberg of the Month." A caption informed me that this recently discovered fatberg in Birmingham measured five meters by five meters by twelve meters and weighed an estimated three tons.

These images were all set on tile walls colored an off-white to match the real-life fatbergs. The floor and even the ceiling were white tile as well. This, a cautionary note on our menus told us, was so that if anyone felt the urge to vomit, they did not have to worry about ruining any paint or carpet. Added to this was a little historical note stating that Fatberger wanted to "revive the legacy of the proud ancient Romans, who would stuff themselves and ease their stomach pain by emptying their stomachs in the *vomitorium*, a special room specifically for throwing up."

There was even a drawing of a Roman *vomitorium*, showing a bunch of rotund Romans eating at an ancient Fatberger and running off to a little side room to spew out their Farty Fries and Atomic Onion Rings. The Fatberger cartoon mascot sat at the head of the table, wearing a toga and stuffing his face with food.

The thing about the *vomitorium* wasn't historically accurate. Yes, I looked it up. *Vomitorium* was, indeed, a real Latin word, but it meant the exits in a stadium that allowed large numbers of people to enter or leave quickly. So it was the stadium vomiting Romans rather than Romans vomiting dormice or starlings' tongues or whatever other strange food they ate.

Convincing Martin of this was another matter.

"No, seriously, look it up," I told him. It was

amazing how much kids were on their phones or computers but never got around to actually researching anything.

"I heard that during big feasts, sometimes they'd go to the *vomitorium* four or five times just so they could eat more," he said, all wide-eyed and eager.

Well, at least it got him interested in ancient history.

We sat in a plus-sized booth with extra-wide seats and looked at our menus, decorated with cartoon fatbergs and drawings of grossly stuffed customers chowing down on greasy meals.

"Hello, young man," Octavian said as he came up to our booth. He was a dapper gentleman about my age. He gave us a big smile to show off his excellent teeth, teeth that, surprisingly enough, were real.

"Hey," Martin mumbled without looking up from his menu.

"And hello to you, pretty lady," he said, giving me a peck on the cheek.

I could just see the top of Martin's forehead over the menu. It turned a deep shade of scarlet.

Octavian cocked his head.

"You've got a tan."

Now it was my turn to blush. "I, um, have been

enjoying the sun a bit lately. It's such a lovely spring."

"I feel jealous. The sun is seeing more of you than I am," he said.

*Oh, if you only knew.*

He sat down beside me and pulled out an iPad. Martin's eye peeked out from behind the menu. How he could have seen the iPad through the menu was a mystery.

"I've been playing a good game with my grand-kids lately," Octavian told him. "Ever tried any of the *Road Rage* series?"

Martin finally showed interest. "Yeah, they're cool."

Octavian fired up his iPad and turned on something called *Road Rage III: Pedestrian Purgatory*. He shifted closer to Martin.

"Okay, so in this game you have to get to work on time through a big traffic jam. You only have five minutes. You lose if you take longer and get bonus points for every second early you are. Let me show you how it's done."

Octavian started the game, and we got a driver's-eye view of a traffic jam. Cars were backed up as far as the eye could see. Octavian immediately pulled onto the sidewalk and hit the gas.

And proceeded to hit a series of pedestrians.

"Cool!" Martin said.

"Now you get points for hitting pedestrians, but you've got to be careful," Octavian explained. "Go for the skinny ones. They don't slow you down as much. Whoa! Almost hit that hot dog stand. Extra points, but I'd have lost five seconds easy. This game is all about balancing out the points you get for hitting people with the points you lose by them slowing you down."

I stared in utter shock. My boyfriend looked like he was actually enjoying this.

Martin sure was. They cheered together as Octavian knocked down a little old lady. I felt left out.

"Why didn't you hit that one?" Martin asked as Octavian swerved around another little old lady, this one hobbling along with the aid of a cane.

"Oh, you have to watch out for those canes. They're a trap. They get stuck on your axle and slow you down for the next twenty seconds. Running over one of them is an easy way to lose the game."

Octavian maneuvered the car among the sidewalk crowd like a pro, avoiding families and old people with canes and sideswiping the skinnier pedestrians when it didn't take him too far out of his way. Sideswiping slowed him down less than actually running people over, and he showed a natural talent for sideswiping.

He made it to the office with fifteen seconds to spare and thirty-eight kills to his tally.

Octavian handed the iPad over to Martin. "Let's see if you can do better."

The waiter came to our booth. He looked about nineteen and was in terrible physical shape. Martin would lose at least a couple of seconds running over him.

"Everybody ready to order?" the waiter asked.

"I'll take the Heart Attack Special with a choco- late milkshake, huge size, and a double order of deep-fried lard chips," Martin said without looking up from his game.

The waiter turned to me.

"I'll take the chicken salad and a soda," I said, bracing for what I knew would come next.

The waiter pulled out a remote from his pocket and pressed the button.

"Wimp menu! Wimp menu!" a speaker at our table blared. A television screen hanging from above our booth turned on, and the cartoon fatberg that was the restaurant chain's mascot appeared. He looked sad and deflated a little.

"Somebody's parents don't know how to get in the spirit of Fatberger," the cartoon blob of fat said in a little squeaky voice. Why would a fatberg have a little squeaky voice? Wouldn't it have a deep voice? Why was I even thinking about this when I had a murder to solve and a restaurant full of people snickering at me for my healthy food choices?

The waiter turned to Octavian.

"And what will you have, sir?"

Octavian stared at the screen, utterly baffled. Obviously he had never been to Fatberger before.

"Sir?" the waiter repeated.

Octavian snapped out of his reverie. "Oh, right. I'll have a cheesesteak and fries."

"Wimp menu! Wimp menu!" the speaker blared again.

Martin rolled his eyes, still playing the game. "You two are so lame."

"I'm lame? You still haven't beat my high score," Octavian said. "Don't run over families. They slow you down too much."

Just as I was about to complain about the boys (not man and boy, but boys) ignoring me, I spotted a pair of familiar faces coming through the door. When I'm in a restaurant or bar, I always get a table with my back to the wall so I can face the door. I've done that all my adult life, and it has only saved me once, in a run-down little cantina in Sonora,

Mexico. Only once in all those years, but once is enough when you consider the alternative.

Now it was paying off again. Perhaps it wasn't saving my life, but seeing who came through that door certainly helped me take several steps forward in the case.

Adrian and Naomi. They came in together and took a booth at the far end.

Fatberger seemed an odd dining choice for a pair of nudists, and I didn't care what they said about body positivity. I suspected they were here because they figured they wouldn't be seen.

I hunched over a little so I wouldn't be visible over the top of our booth, which had fairly high-backed seats. I peeked over and saw they were in an animated conversation. Adrian kept gesturing to her, and Naomi sat slumped, shaking her head. Neither looked around, figuring no other nudist would come to such a place.

I wouldn't have been here either except for Martin.

The waiter approached their table, and I ducked before they looked up. I could hear them talking, but they were too far away for me to hear what they said.

"Wimp menu! Wimp menu!" their speaker blared a moment later.

All right, so maybe they were trying to cut down the calories after all.

Good thing I had made myself scarce. I was sure they were looking around nervously at that very moment. Nothing like becoming the center of attention when one was trying to be sneaky.

But sneaky about what?

Luckily Martin wanted to stay for dessert—a Super Sludge Sundae with deep-fried whipped cream—and took his time eating because of those pesky pedestrians he had to kill, so Adrian and Naomi left before we had to stand up and make ourselves visible.

I had heard nothing of their conversation and seen nothing more than Adrian insisting on something and Naomi looking dubious. Just before they left, Adrian slipped an envelope over to her. She paused, nodded, and put it in her purse.

They left separately.

Now my curiosity was piqued. Whatever was going on over at Sunnydale, it had to do with taxes. It baffled me that the IRS specialists hadn't spotted anything. Those bloodhounds have eagle eyes when they catch the scent of financial wrongdoing, and not even a mixed metaphor will stop them.

I decided I needed to pay Sunnydale Nature Resort a nocturnal visit.

## THIRTEEN

I had, of course, scouted out the resort already using Google Earth and had discovered a small dirt road that skirted the woods at the northern edge of the property. I could find a place to park there and cut through the woods easily enough.

The only problem was that I'd heard Adrian and Zoe lived on the property. There were no facilities for overnight guests, at least, but I'd have to take care.

After dropping a bloated Martin off at his parents' house and wishing him a good night, I headed back out into the countryside. I felt a bit bloated myself. Even the salads at Fatberger came with dollops of mayonnaise and creamy dressing, and the chicken turned out to be deep fried.

Whoever heard of putting fried chicken in a chicken salad?

I found the dirt road easily enough, cutting past a farm just a mile ahead of the Sunnydale entrance. Luckily, no other cars passed by, so no one saw me pull off onto what turned out to be a rutted, over-grown, and disused dirt track. Trees pressed in on the left side, their branches scraping against the doors, and the wheel ruts were so deep from the tractors that came along this way that the central hump kept grinding against the bottom of the car.

The road had looked better from the satellite pictures offered by Google. My rental car bumped and scraped its way along, and I could practically hear my security deposit disappearing with every clonk and bang and screech.

The bumps squeezed out a few burps from yours truly, courtesy of Fatberger. I pictured Martin laughing hysterically at me. That's what he had done the last time we had gone there and the food had had this effect. He had probably been hoping for a repeat performance.

After a mile or so, I estimated I was parallel to the Sunnydale property and parked right in the lane. I hadn't seen any place to turn off, and I figured there was little chance of anyone else passing by here at this hour.

I got out, geared up for a night of fun. I wore a black shirt and loose black pants and had a balaclava I could put over my face. I had my 9mm and pepper spray, of course, plus a small bag holding a Mini Maglite, my lockpicks, my phone, and a pair of bolt cutters.

The bolt cutters were because I had seen what looked like a chain link fence around the boundary of the nudist colony. While the property was ringed with trees, there were a few bare spots where I could see a thin gray line.

It's amazing what you can find on Google Earth, and most people only use it to find the closest Starbucks.

I pushed my way through the trees, my Maglite showing me the way. I found the fence not far in. Peering through the links, I could see the trees continued for a way beyond.

Good. No one would see my light. I got to work on the fence.

And it got to work on me. There was a time when I could snip through a double coil of razor wire and make an adult-sized crawlspace within five minutes and do it quietly.

Not anymore. Here I was faced with a simple chain link fence, each bit of wire conveniently held taught by the network of its neighbors and safely smooth, not some bobbing, shivering, razor-sharp coil of military-grade defensive wire, and it was taking me ages.

I hadn't gotten a quarter of the way through before I began to feel every snip of the wire in my finger joints. Something about the pressure and sudden release as the metal gave hurt me terribly.

I stopped when I got a third of the way through. My intent had been to cut a simple hole that I could duck through. I should have been done by now, and instead I was looking at less than a half circle of cut fence. I rubbed my joints, frustrated.

Continuing, I didn't get more than ten links cut before I had to stop again.

I stepped back, wincing with pain and looking at the fence with despair.

This place … this place … it was hitting me on every level. Having to show my body to strangers, having to interact in an atmosphere that was weirdly pseudo-sexual (at least to me), and now this new reminder of the ravages of time. Yet another thing I couldn't do. I probably hadn't cut any wire since Somalia in the nineties. The ability was one of those things I had thought would always be there, like James or being able to see the sights on my gun without my reading glasses. Another bit of my old life I had taken for granted. Gone.

I glared at the fence and said something unprintable.

Getting back to work with gritted teeth, pain lancing through my forearms now with each snip of the wire, I soldiered on through until I'd cut the hole I had set out to make.

At last the final wire sheared away and the circle of fence fell into the underbrush. I ducked through, gave it a kick, and stowed my bolt cutters. It took me three attempts to get them into my bag.

I allowed myself a little cry over James. Any time something like this happened, it made me miss him more. I think growing old would be much easier to bear if I had someone to grumble with. Frederick and Alicia and Martin were a blessing in my life, but they had lives and futures of their own. While I didn't have to grow old alone, I was alone in growing old.

Okay, enough of that.

I wiped my eyes, squared my shoulders, and got on with the mission.

It didn't take long to creep through the screen of trees and into a field beyond. I came out past the pool and activity building, visible in the far distance and illuminated by a couple of outside lights. The office, my goal, lay hidden behind them. I threw some sticks on the grass in a seemingly random pattern so I could find my escape route.

I hid in the shadow of the tree line, watching for several minutes. No sound but the cicadas. No movement. The interior lights were all off in the activity center.

The tricky thing was that Adrian and Zoe had their little house right behind the office. I could only hope they weren't working late. I pulled my balaclava over my face.

My luck held as I crossed the field, silent and nearly invisible in my black clothing.

I stopped with my back pressed against the wall of the activity center, listening. Still no sound. Peering through a window, I didn't see any signs of life inside. Good. No nocturnal activities in the activity room. The last thing I needed tonight was to come across a pair of amorous nudists being positive about each other's bodies.

I was not a prude, really, but I just wanted this mission over without having to deal with any more embarrassments.

Yeah, like that was going to happen.

I crept around the corner of the activity center and studied the office and house behind. The office was dark. In the house, a light shone downstairs. It was too far away to see anything clearly. The night air brought the faint sound of a television. Good, the sound would mask my movements. Bad, because they obviously had a window open.

Speed was the answer, speed I didn't have. In the old days, I would have run low and silently to the office and quickly gotten out of sight of that window. Instead I walked quickly and silently and eventually got out of sight.

No one appeared at that window. No one shouted. Thank goodness for the apathetic American television viewer, clothed or otherwise.

I dared a quick shine of my light and saw no stickers warning of a security system. I saw no telltale wires either, and I did not recall seeing a keypad inside the front door like I had in my own home.

The door was locked, of course, but I took care of that with my lockpicks easily enough. I allowed myself a smile. That was something time hadn't yet stolen from me.

I eased the door open and closed it silently behind me. The interior of the office was dark, the Venetian blinds all closed. I turned my Maglite back on, half covering it with my hand. With the feeble glow I allowed through my fingers, I made my way to Adrian's desk. The desktop had a photo of him and Zoe in the buff at a beach somewhere, a landline phone, and a few papers having to do with some plumbing repair in the activity center. There was also a desktop computer on sleep mode. I didn't touch that, figuring there'd be a password.

Holding the Maglite in my mouth, I began to rummage through his drawers.

Searching files in the dark was not really my specialty. I was more on the covert ops side of things, not domestic spying. It took me some time to find a file marked "Taxes—Personal."

That set off a little bell in my head. Grimal had only mentioned checking the resort's tax returns, not Adrian and Zoe's personal returns, on the assumption that any financial malfeasance would happen with the resort's finances. But what if…?

Bingo. It turned out that Adrian had a private income. He owned two apartment buildings down in Georgia and earned a considerable amount of money from rents. I found receipts for rents, repairs, payment to the building manager, plus tax returns going back ten years. I wondered where he had gotten the money to buy two buildings. Had he inherited them, or had he come by them in a more dubious fashion?

The tax forms might have been written in Babylonian cuneiform for all I could understand them. I've always hated doing my taxes and always hired an accountant to do them for me. What I did see was that the income derived from the apartment buildings stayed more or less constant throughout the last ten years except for three years ago, when the income jumped by about ten percent. The receipts showed he had raised the rent. In the line for "tax preparer," I saw Clarissa Monell's signature on the most recent eight years.

I put that file away and found another folder that was unmarked. This contained returns for the upcoming year, filled out in pencil with many notes in the margins. It was in a different handwriting that I assumed was Naomi's.

The first form showed an income on the apartment buildings that was about ten percent less than the previous year, even though receipts showed he had raised the rent again. In a different handwriting on the margin was a big "NO!" with a circle around it. Unlike the handwriting that filled out the form, this looked to have been written by a male hand. Adrian not approving of Naomi's numbers?

Another form showed an even lower figure. In the margins in the same male hand was the word "Better."

Then it clicked. Adrian was trying to fudge his personal taxes. He wanted to hide the fact that he was making more income. Naomi seemed reluctant to play along with the game, and perhaps Clarissa had out and out refused.

Had Clarissa threatened to spill the beans to the IRS? That could lead Adrian to murder. It seemed a bit of a crazy reason to kill, however. We were only talking about a few tens of thousands of dollars in tax here. Unless there was something else involved. Perhaps it wasn't so much the hiding of the income that Adrian wanted to cover up but what he planned to do with it.

I let out a celebratory Fatberger belch that tasted of half-digested fried chicken. I was much closer to a solution than before. It was amazing what a little illegal breaking and entering could bring to a case.

I dug deeper into the drawers and found little else, just older files relating to the resort and a plaque from Boeing dated from twenty-five years ago naming Adrian Fletcher "Engineer of the Year." So he had been an engineer at a big military contractor before owning a nudist camp. Those jobs paid well, and he had given it all up to invest in a nudist colony next to a conservative town. Quite a gamble. He meant all that stuff he said about his dedication to nudism.

I replaced the files the way I had found them

and closed the drawers. Now I had a motive. What I needed was proof.

Checking the other desk, I found it was Naomi's and didn't see anything amiss inside.

The small office building had a second room, reached through an open doorway. I found a pair of file cabinets, a closet full of office supplies, and another closet with various tools, sports equipment, and other odds and ends.

I let out another belch and got a bitter taste in my mouth. A burning in my chest reminded me that I should have brought my antacids. A few minutes of searching turned up nothing of use.

Just as I turned to go back into the main room for another look, I heard footsteps outside. I turned off my Maglite and ducked behind the doorway, cursing my luck. I was out of sight of the main room, but if whoever it was came in here, I would have nowhere to hide.

Of course, they'd get a gun pointed at their face, but I would rather settle this without violence. I'd been in too many gunfights in my so-called retirement already.

I heard a key go into the lock, and the door opened.

"Damn it, Zoe."

That had been Adrian's voice. No doubt he had

noticed the door was unlocked and had assumed Zoe had forgotten to lock it. The way he said it made it sound like he habitually blamed Zoe for a lot of things.

The light turned on, and the door closed. Footsteps crossed the room. I heard him sit down and pick up the landline phone on his desk.

A minute later, Adrian spoke again.

"Hey, baby, I can only talk for a minute."

Pause.

"Yeah, good to hear your voice too. I know, I know. But I couldn't help it. Naming you to the post means I get to spend more time with you."

Pause.

"I know people are talking. It won't matter for long. Soon we'll get out of here. The taxes are getting all fixed up. We'll have enough."

Pause.

"Wherever you want. Yeah, I've heard the resorts in the south of France are wonderful. Yes, I looked at the links you sent me. That will be great."

Pause.

"I told you we'll have enough money. Don't worry."

Pause.

"Okay. Don't worry. Everything's going to be fine. Look, I got to go. I told her I just needed to fix one thing on a spreadsheet. She'll be wondering where I am. See you tomorrow? Great."

Pause.

"Yes, yes. She's come around. I told you, everything will be fine."

Pause.

"Love you too, Angie. Bye bye."

He hung up. I heard him cross the room again and open the door.

My stomach knotted. An acidic burn rose in my throat. Ugh, why did I let Martin convince me to go to Fatberger? I was going to have an uncomfortable night.

It suddenly got more uncomfortable.

Before I could stop it, a loud belch erupted from my throat.

## FOURTEEN

"Who's there?" Adrian demanded.

The game was up. I stepped out from behind the doorway, gun leveled.

Adrian stood at the front door, his hand on the knob, the door half open. Luckily for me he had his clothes on.

At my appearance, he let out a little squawk.

"Who are you? What do you want?"

What, didn't he recognize me with my clothes on?

Oh, the balaclava. I pulled it off my face.

"Barbara? What's going on?"

"Keep your voice down." I motioned with my gun. "Sit down in that chair while I call the police."

He looked baffled. "Police? What for? You're the one breaking into my office!"

"For the murder of Clarissa Monell."

"What? That was a hit and run. Why do you think I killed her?"

"Because she wouldn't doctor your taxes, and you're obviously about to elope with Angie."

"I'd never kill anyone."

Then something clicked. Adrian had been a mechanical engineer. He could have figured out a better way to pick my lock than with a paperclip. And look at him shaking head to toe at the sight of a gun. Was this a cold-blooded killer?

"You pressured Clarissa to fudge your taxes, and she wouldn't do it," I said. "Don't try to lie. I just saw your old tax returns, plus the new ones Naomi is doctoring."

He hung his head. After a pause, he whispered, "Yes, it's true. I pressured Clarissa, and she wouldn't budge. It stressed her out and ruined our friendship. Eventually she quit, and I got Naomi to do the taxes. She didn't want to change them either, but I convinced her. She's more pliable than Clarissa." His head came up, eyes desperate. "But I didn't kill her, I swear. Why would I do that? She never threatened me. Are you saying that it wasn't a hit and run?"

"I saw it with my own eyes. A stolen car pulled out of a parking spot and deliberately ran her over.

The driver also tried to run me off the road when I pursued."

"Pursued? Who are you?"

"Never mind that. So when were you planning on eloping with Angie?"

"Soon. She was worried about money. She's always worried about money. She grew up poor, you see."

"And she's still worried that you don't have enough." The final piece clicked. It was Angie who had killed Clarissa. It was the only solution. But why? If Clarissa hadn't been threatening to expose them, what was the danger?

"Where's Angie now?" I asked.

"At home."

"You got your car keys?"

"What? No, they're in the house."

"Fine, we'll go in my car."

"But Zoe will notice I'm gone."

I shrugged. "You were going to leave her anyway. Move it."

I gestured with my gun, and he got up. He put his hands in the air, and we walked out of the office. I turned the light off in case Zoe peeked out. I didn't want her to see me leading her husband away. She should be spared that much, at least.

"Why do we need to go to Angie's?" he asked.

I shook my head. He still didn't get it, did he? Not that I entirely got it either. That was why we needed to pay her a visit. She must be the murderer, but why she had killed was not yet clear.

We walked across the field. When we were halfway to the tree line, I heard Zoe's voice far behind us, calling Adrian's name. Adrian stopped and turned.

"Keep moving. She can't see us from there."

"Please don't do this. All I want is to be happy."

"Zoe seems like a nice woman. Why can't you be content with her?"

He didn't answer. I shook my head in disgust. The same old story—trading the wife in for a newer model. Disgusting. I let out a Fatberger belch to show my feelings.

Zoe's calls followed us to the trees.

We passed through, Adrian cursing when he saw the hole I'd cut in his fence, and I led him to the car. At gunpoint I buckled him in to the passenger's seat, strapping the seatbelt over his arms and making him sit on his hands. I should have brought some handcuffs along.

My car nearly got stuck as I tried to do a three-point turn to head back the way I had come. The dirt track was too narrow, hemmed in by trees on one side and mud on the other. My three-point turn became a twelve-point turn. At least Adrian didn't crack a joke about women drivers. I might have slugged him. I didn't like slugging people anymore. It hurt my hand.

Turned out I had to slug him after all.

When we made it off the track and were on the road heading for town, he let out a shriek that sounded something like "You won't take my Angie away from me!" but came out more like "Yoooarggghangieme!!!!", wriggled his arms out of his seatbelt, and grabbed the steering wheel.

Remember what I said about how every layer of safety, no matter how thin, can be lifesaving? That trick with the seatbelt saved both our lives.

The two seconds it took for him to get his arms free allowed me to grip the steering wheel tighter, pull my gun out, and smack him across the temple with it.

Even so, he managed to grab the wheel and swerve us enough that the side of the rental car ground against the margin barrier. If he had gotten the chance, he would have probably made us go right through the thing.

I hit him again, and he calmed down, and by calmed down I mean he cradled his head and rocked back and forth, moaning.

"You really are quite a poor excuse for a human

being, aren't you?" I said. "Now sit quiet, or I'll shoot you."

Of course, I really wouldn't have shot him. Just pistol-whipped him a few more times.

Amid sobs and pleas for mercy, he led me to Angie's house. It was a cute little bungalow in the cheaper part of town, although no part of Cheerville was by any means cheap. I didn't know why Angie was fussing about money.

"What does Angie do for a living?"

"She's the manager of a motorcycle shop on the highway," Adrian replied.

I shrugged. Solid middle-class living. A house in a nice town. Friends. Beauty. And she wanted to run off with this guy?

Angie must have heard us park in the driveway, right behind her sporty yellow Kawasaki, because she opened the door just as we came up her front steps.

She saw the bruises on her boyfriend's face, the stern look on mine, and the suspicious gun-shaped bulge in my right pocket and did the math.

Angie slumped.

"Come on in," she mumbled.

We followed her inside. She sat heavily in an armchair in the front room. Adrian went to her and put his arms around her. I remained standing by the door.

I cut to the quick.

"So why did you do it?" I asked. "And don't lie. I know about the doctored tax forms, and I know about the two of you planning to elope."

I wanted this to be over. My hands were still sore from cutting through the fence, I was sleepy, and I had a terrible case of heartburn. I felt if I belched again, I might burn the house down.

These two would probably deserve that.

"She was going to tell Zoe," Angie whispered, looking down at the floor. She resembled nothing more than a chastened schoolchild.

Adrian clutched at her. "No, don't tell me that! You didn't! Tell me you didn't!"

Angie didn't reply. I could see realization dawning on Adrian's face. He pulled his hands away like he had suddenly realized he was touching a snake.

"She was my friend," he moaned.

I remembered the photo of him with his arm around Clarissa and Zoe leaning away from them, and I wondered if she had been something more.

Angie looked at him. "She had started to hate you. She told me she lost a lot of respect for you when you pressured her to change the taxes. She tried to turn me against you. I think she was jealous. When I wouldn't listen, she threatened to call the IRS. She didn't have the guts to threaten you to your face, so she threatened me. You would have gone to jail. Naomi would have gone to jail. It would have ruined everything. I did it to protect you."

Angie turned and glared at me. "If it wasn't for you, a week from now, we could have been sunning ourselves in a nudist resort in the south of France. We had enough to live for a couple of years, and Adrian had found out a good way to dodge taxes. We could have lived on his rental income. I could have ridden in the European circuit. We could have been happy."

I felt sick, and not just from the junk food I had eaten for dinner. So this was it. A bright, popular woman had been run down in the street for no other crime than being honest and endangering the happiness of two selfish people. Now Clarissa was gone, and Adrian's life was wrecked from the guilt I could see in his tortured features, and Zoe's life would be ruined too. Naomi would get in trouble, and the entire community of Sunnydale was in mourning over the loss of its most popular member. The scandal might even cause the place to close.

Oddly, I felt sad that Sunnydale might be no

more. It wasn't my kind of community, but it was a community, with all its friendships and jokes and fun.

And its seamy underside.

"One thing I don't get. When you tried to run me off the road, you did it like an amateur. I initially ruled you out as a suspect because of that."

Angie shook her head. "I never meant to run you off the road, only scare you. Once you backed off, I took my chance to get away."

Adrian was sitting on the floor, weeping. I looked at him with pity…

…and didn't see the lamp being thrown at me until it was almost too late.

I dodged, and the lamp that had been aimed at my head only struck my shoulder, causing me to drop my gun. Angie scooped up a set of keys on the side table and bolted for the door. I managed to trip her on her way out. She stumbled down the steps, picked herself up, and ran for her motorcycle.

I grabbed my gun.

"Stop right there!" I shouted.

"No!" Adrian tried to tackle me. An elbow to the gut stopped that move. His gut was soft enough that I didn't even hurt my elbow.

By time time, Angie had leaped onto her motor-cycle, fired it up, and peeled out across her front lawn. I leveled my pistol. Even though I didn't have my glasses on and couldn't see the sights properly, it was an easy shot.

A shot I didn't take. I couldn't gun down this overgrown child. Let the police track her down.

She revved the motorcycle and tore down the street. Just then, a car turned the corner and screeched to a stop sideways across the road, blocking it.

Angie tried to swerve, but it was too late. She ended up skidding out and falling away from her motorcycle, tucking into a roll but no doubt getting more of that "road rash" she had suffered in another accident. She ended up several yards down the street, moaning but alive. I hurried toward her, Adrian close behind.

The door to the car opened, and a woman stepped out.

Liz.

I stopped in front of her as Adrian rushed to Angie's side.

"You followed me again," I said.

"That's right," Liz said, giving me a cheeky grin.

"And I didn't spot you. That's twice. No one has ever done that to me twice. You have skills beyond the training of an artillery observer. Just who are you?"

"Never mind me," she said, aping my own words to her during our previous conversation. "Did you get a confession?"

"It was Angie, not Adrian."

Liz nodded. "She hero worshipped him. Many of the girls do. I'd heard rumors of their affair but thought it was just talk. Today I dug a little deeper and found out it was all true. I was going to tell you, but I guess you have this case just about wrapped up."

"Thank goodness," I said, looking at Angie. She didn't seem too badly hurt. "Now I can go back to a nice, quiet retirement."

Liz laughed. "Don't try that sweet little grand-mother act with me. I don't buy it for a second."

"And I don't buy that you're a former artillery observer and now just a peaceful, ordinary citizen."

Our gaze held for a moment. She was the first to break it.

"I'll call the cops," she said, turning away from me and pulling out her phone.

## FIFTEEN

Two days later, I was enjoying a nice cup of tea at home. My sunburn had gone away, and I could sit fully clothed in the privacy of my own home. I felt a profound sense of relief.

I had let Grimal tie up the loose ends and take the credit, as usual. Angie's confession to me had landed her in jail, and while she had hired an attorney, things looked pretty bad for her. Adrian had suffered a nervous breakdown and confessed to his plans to dodge taxes and run away with her. Naomi had confessed to helping him with the taxes. The thing was, since they hadn't yet sent in that tax return, there was only conspiracy to commit tax fraud rather than tax fraud itself. I suspected both would get off in exchange for help in prosecuting Angie.

Grimal had been grateful for my help, and while he wasn't decent enough to thank me, he did say the police department would pay for the damage to the rental car.

I decided not to tell him about that envelope I had seen Adrian slip Naomi. I suspected it had been a bribe. Proving it would be difficult, and I didn't want Naomi to get into any more trouble. She had made a foolish mistake while under Adrian's sway, and the embarrassment and publicity were punishment enough. The important thing was that we had caught Clarissa's killer.

The case was splashed across the local papers and even made the statewide papers thanks to the nudism angle. Many in Cheerville expressed surprise that there was a nudist colony just outside of town. I hoped there wouldn't be a public backlash. Towns like Cheerville can be terribly conservative, at least on the outside, and it would be a pity if Sunnydale Nature Resort got run out of the area.

My phone rang, and I picked it up.

"Hey, Barbara, it's Liz."

"Well, if it isn't my favorite nudist mystery woman. How are things up at Sunnydale?"

I had been avoiding the place ever since I broke the case. My naturism had come to its natural conclusion. I'm not a prude, but there are limits.

"Everything's crazy up here. Zoe is filing for divorce and plans to buy out Adrian's portion of the resort. The members have set up a crowdfunding campaign to help her. He hasn't dared show his face around here. Neither has Naomi. Needless to say, Zoe is livid with her. Things are going better than expected, though."

"Better than expected? Really?"

"Oh yes. The publicity has been great. We've had a boom in membership applications. Some are creepy guys we have to turn away, of course, but many are good people who have read up on what nudism is all about and want to give it a try."

"I suppose there's going to be a run on Sun Shield lotion."

Liz laughed. "I hope so. We don't want a bunch of lobsters running around like you were."

I laughed too. After a pause, Liz went on.

"We haven't seen you up there for the past couple of days."

I shifted in my seat. "Yes, I'm sorry to have deceived you by infiltrating your community, but I did it with the best of intentions."

"You got justice for Clarissa. Everyone understands. We miss you, though. People like you up here, and you're the heroine of the hour. How about you come on up tomorrow?"

"That's very kind of you, but to be honest, it's not really my kind of place."

"I see. Would you like to have a coffee tomorrow instead? You're an interesting woman, Barbara, and I'd like to learn more about you."

"I bet you would. I'd like to learn more about you too."

There was a pause on the line.

"How about we talk about the weather and books instead?"

"That might be better."

"Deal?"

"Deal."

After seeing Liz's skill set, I didn't believe she had been a forward observer for the Army. A forward observer is positioned as close to enemy lines as possible in order to call in locations for the artillery to hit. With her level of ability, I thought she was a bit closer to enemy lines than that. I think she was actually behind enemy lines.

Not that I'd ever get her to admit it.

She could be a useful ally, though. This sleepy little town was turning out to be quite lively, and I could use more allies than just the bumbling likes of Police Chief Arnold Grimal.

And I could always use another friend.

"It's a date. I'll talk to you later, Liz. I think I

hear my son pulling up. He's dropping off my grandson. He's going to stay with me for a couple of hours. Bye now."

"Bye."

I heard my grandson running up the walkway, followed quickly by a loud pounding on my door. Why do teenagers always sound like a SWAT team about to break your door in?

"Coming!" I called.

As soon as I opened the door, Dandelion shot between my legs and clawed her way up Martin until she was snuggled in his arms.

"Hi, Grandma! What's for dinner?"

"Hello to you too. I'm ordering Chinese."

He looked at me. "No Fatberger?"

"I can't take that more than once a month. Once a lifetime would be preferable."

"Oh well," Martin said, scratching Dandelion behind the ears as she purred contentedly.

He walked over to my sofa, about to plop down in his usual spot and turn on the TV, when he stopped. His jaw dropped. His arms fell to his sides. Dandelion held on to his shirt for a moment or two, then jumped off and ran away.

"What's the matter?" I asked.

Then I followed his gaze.

On the side table next to the sofa were the

brochures Adrian and Zoe had given me—"The ABCs of Nudism," "Nudism for all Ages," and "Political Naturism: How We Can Bring Peace to the World Through a Clothing-Free Lifestyle." Beside them was the latest issue of the glossy magazine *Naturism Monthly*.

Martin turned to me with a look of utter horror. It was beyond shock—it was the soul-rending terror of gazing into the darkest abyss of existence and having it gaze back at you. It was the nihilistic agony of knowing that all your reality has been shattered.

He looked at me, his aged grandmother, that kindly old woman who bought him cookies … and saw a nudist.

"It's not what you think," I said, hearing how lame my words sounded.

His eyes widened. If it wasn't what he thought, it must be worse than he thought!

"Can you keep a secret?" I asked.

Martin shook his head, and again I realized I had said precisely the wrong thing. I needed to fix this situation immediately.

"I    was    …    helping    with    a    murder investigation."

That caught him off guard.

"Huh?"

"Did you hear about the murder at the nudist colony?"

"Yeah," he said in a guarded tone.

"I helped find the murderer. I'm not a nudist. I infiltrated the nudist colony to help the police because they would never suspect me."

"Huh?" Now Martin was utterly confused. He didn't even notice Dandelion had gotten into an epic war with his shoelaces and was losing.

"Sit down, Martin, and we'll have a little chat. There are some things you don't know about Grandma."

Harper Lin is the *USA TODAY* bestselling author of 6 cozy mystery series including *The Patisserie Mysteries* and *The Cape Bay Cafe Mysteries*.

When she's not reading or writing mysteries, she loves going to yoga classes, hiking, and hanging out with her family and friends.

For a complete list of her books by series, visit her website.

www.HarperLin.com

**MYSTERY LIN**

**Lin, Harper**
**Granny bares it all :**
**a secret agent granny**

**11/15/18**

CPSIA information can be obtained
at www.ICGtesting.com
Printed in the USA
LVHW03s1123211018
594316LV00003B/388/P

9 781987 859614